RIDE TO LIVE

Harold thrust his bloody hand at Fargo, displaying the stub of his finger. "Forget *this*? Forget what they have done to me? Mister, I owe them Apaches, and if it's the last thing I ever do, I will make them pay."

Fargo had heard similar bluster before and gave it no more heed than worthless hot air was due. "Right now we need to think about putting more distance between them and us. We're not safe until we're sure we have shaken them." Fargo was fairly certain the five warriors had not come after them, but then again, Apaches were notoriously unpredictable.

"My son needs rest," George Haxton said.

"He can get all the sleep he wants when we stop for the night," Fargo responded. "We do this my way, or I ride off and leave you. I won't let your stupidity get me killed."

George did not hide his disgust. "I don't think I like you very much."

"I do," Patricia said, smiling sweetly. "I like Mr. Fargo a whole lot. Let's do as he says and everything will be all right."

"All right?" Fargo grimly shook his head. "Hell, girl. We'll be lu___ __ ___ out of this alive."

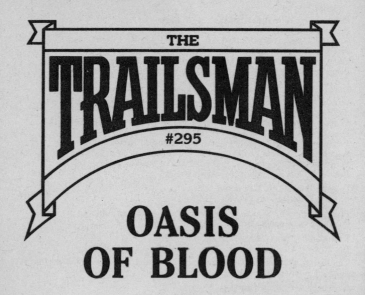

THE TRAILSMAN
#295

OASIS
OF BLOOD

by

Jon Sharpe

A SIGNET BOOK

SIGNET
Published by New American Library, a division of
Penguin Group (USA) Inc., 375 Hudson Street,
New York, New York 10014, USA
Penguin Group (Canada), 90 Eglinton Avenue East, Suite 700, Toronto,
Ontario M4P 2Y3, Canada (a division of Pearson Penguin Canada Inc.)
Penguin Books Ltd., 80 Strand, London WC2R 0RL, England
Penguin Ireland, 25 St. Stephen's Green, Dublin 2,
Ireland (a division of Penguin Books Ltd.)
Penguin Group (Australia), 250 Camberwell Road, Camberwell, Victoria 3124,
Australia (a division of Pearson Australia Group Pty. Ltd.)
Penguin Books India Pvt. Ltd., 11 Community Centre, Panchsheel Park,
New Delhi - 110 017, India
Penguin Group (NZ), cnr Airborne and Rosedale Roads, Albany,
Auckland 1310, New Zealand (a division of Pearson New Zealand Ltd.)
Penguin Books (South Africa) (Pty.) Ltd., 24 Sturdee Avenue,
Rosebank, Johannesburg 2196, South Africa

Penguin Books Ltd., Registered Offices:
80 Strand, London WC2R 0RL, England

First published by Signet, an imprint of New American Library,
a division of Penguin Group (USA) Inc.

First Printing, May 2006
10 9 8 7 6 5 4 3 2 1

The first chapter of this book previously appeared in *Oregon Outlaws*, the two
hundred ninety-fourth volume in this series.

Copyright © Penguin Group (USA) Inc., 2006
All rights reserved

 REGISTERED TRADEMARK—MARCA REGISTRADA

Printed in the United States of America

PUBLISHER'S NOTE
This is a work of fiction. Names, characters, places, and incidents either are the
product of the author's imagination or are used fictitiously, and any resemblance
to actual persons, living or dead, events, or locales is entirely coincidental.

   The publisher does not have any control over and does not assume any respon-
sibility for author or third-party Web sites or their content.

The Trailsman

Beginnings . . . they bend the tree and they mark the man. Skye Fargo was born when he was eighteen. Terror was his midwife, vengeance his first cry. Killing spawned Skye Fargo, ruthless, cold-blooded murder. Out of the acrid smoke of gunpowder still hanging in the air, he rose, cried out a promise never forgotten.

The Trailsman they began to call him all across the West: searcher, scout, hunter, the man who could see where others only looked, his skills for hire but not his soul, the man who lived each day to the fullest, yet trailed each tomorrow. Skye Fargo, the Trailsman, the seeker who could take the wildness of a land and the wanting of a woman and make them his own.

*New Mexico Territory, 1861—where hate burns
hotter than the sun and blood
flows more deeply than the rivers.*

1

He came on the Apaches by chance. That was often the way. When Apaches did not want to be seen or heard they moved as silently as ghosts. But even Apaches did not have eyes in the backs of their heads. It helped that the three warriors were intent on something or someone up ahead.

Luck was with Skye Fargo. But then, he had always been lucky at cards, even more lucky with women, and lucky, too, when it mattered most, when his life was in the balance. Better lucky than rich, someone once said, and Fargo wouldn't disagree, although he would not mind having a lot of money. Too often a few cold cards made up for a lot of hot cards, and women and fine whiskey were expensive propositions in their own right. What money he did earn or win he spent almost as soon as he earned or won it. Small wonder he usually had little to his name.

On this blistering hot afternoon, as Fargo alertly wound south through the heart of New Mexico Territory, he had been thinking about a certain dove in Denver who had insisted on hiring a carriage for a ride up into the foothills under the full moon, when he was rudely jarred out of his reverie by the sight of a moccasin print in the dirt not three feet in front of his Ovaro. In a twinkling, his Colt was in his hand, and he reined up.

Fargo scanned his immediate vicinity. The arid landscape baked by the sun betrayed no hint of life. It had been hours since he came across so much as a lizard. An oppressive silence reigned, alleviated all too infrequently by a vagrant whisper of welcome breeze.

Dismounting, Fargo held on to the pinto's reins, and hunkered down. Once again, he had been lucky. The track was fresh. It was rare for Apaches to blunder like this. Normally, they were as adept as foxes at hiding their sign. He searched but found no more prints. Still, one track was warning enough.

Twirling the Colt into its holster, Fargo gripped the saddle horn and swung back up. He gigged the Ovaro, holding to a walk, his hand on the Colt. A tall man, broad of shoulder and deep of chest, he wore buckskins and boots and favored a red bandanna. His white hat, like the rest of him, was so caked with dust that it was no longer white but the color of the dirt under his mount's heavy hooves. He had piercing lake blue eyes, and now those eyes roved ceaselessly in search of the maker of that track, and any friends the maker might have.

The army had warned him. The mission they had sent him on was fraught with peril. He would learn the details once he arrived at Fort Craig. It was sufficient to know he must travel through Apache country.

Apaches held no love for the white man. Unlike the Shoshones and the Crows, who had welcomed the white tide with open arms, the Apaches resented the invasion of their territory—resented it with all the inborn pride of their independent spirits. They resented the whites just as they had resented the Mexicans before them, and the Spaniards before the Mexicans. But they were fair in their resentments. They waged war on other tribes, as well. To the Apaches, everyone else was an enemy, and enemies were to be killed or plundered.

Fargo was not one of those whites who hated Apaches, or Indians in general, for hatred's sake. He admired anyone, white, red, or otherwise, who stood up for what was theirs. But he had been born white, and that made him their enemy, whether he wanted to be or not. They would kill him on sight, or try to.

As circumstance would have it, Fargo and the Apache,

or Apaches, ahead of him were winding down a broad canyon. He was above them. When he came to a shelf overlooking the canyon floor, he reined up well back from the rim, slid down, and crept to the edge. It was well he exercised caution, for there, only two hundred yards below, was the maker of the track and his four dusky companions. They were dressed in breechclouts and knee-high moccasins. Only one wore a shirt. All carried rifles and wore cartridge belts. All had long knives at their hips. Like hungry wolves that had caught the scent of prey, they flitted from boulder to boulder and cranny to cranny. Clearly, they were stalking someone.

Then Fargo saw a thin tendril of smoke rise half a mile lower down. Squinting against the glare, he saw three horses, and figures around a campfire, and wondered who in God's name had been so stupid as to make camp out in the open in the middle of the day in the heart of Apache country. They had to be white, and they had to be new to New Mexico. They would not live to grow old, as careless as they were.

Fargo swore under his breath. This was the last thing he needed. By rights he should ride on and leave the idiots to their fate. But the thought of what the Apaches would do if the warriors took any of them alive was enough to make him remount and cautiously work his way lower.

He had to be extremely careful. He must not show himself, nor let the Ovaro be seen or heard. Fortunately, there was plenty of cover, huge boulders and the like that he used to his best advantage. He had another advantage, as well. He was on horseback, and the Apaches were on foot. Accordingly, he reined sharply to the east, swinging wide of the five warriors, and once he was sure he was out of their hearing, he applied his spurs and raced like the devil for the canyon floor and the fools and their fire.

The Apaches would spot him once he broke into the open. That could not be helped. Fargo forestalled the inevitable as long as he could. Only when he was almost to the bottom did he leave cover. He could well imagine the Apaches' surprise. It was matched by the surprise of the three people who rose and turned toward him as he approached at a gallop.

Sure enough, they were white. Two were men in homespun: big, brawny sorts who had the look of farmers. The third, to Fargo's extreme annoyance, was a woman. But what a woman! Lustrous chestnut hair framed a lovely oval face. Hazel eyes regarded him with interest as he came to a stop in a swirling cloud of dust. A homespun dress, molded to her form, hinted at a ripe bounty underneath. Her lips were red and full, twin cherries. She was, in short, a vision who would stir the most chaste of men, and Fargo was far from chaste.

The older of the men, who had to be pushing fifty, smiled, but did not lower the rifle he had raised. "How do you do, friend? You seem to be in a hurry." He had an oxlike build and a great oxlike head. Even his large brown eyes had an oxlike quality to them.

Fargo had no time for pleasantries. "What the hell are you doing here?"

The man blinked. "I beg your pardon?"

"You heard me." Fargo gestured at their fire. A coffeepot had been set on to boil. Their horses had been stripped, and their saddles and saddle blankets spread out. "It's too damn early to stop for the day."

"I will thank you," the man said peckishly, "not to use crude language in the presence of a lady."

"My crude language is the least of your worries," Fargo snapped. "Apaches have taken an interest in you." He glanced up the canyon but did not see them, which was to be expected.

The younger man, whose features were similar enough to the older to mark him as the man's son, had his cheek pressed to the stock of a Sharps. "We haven't seen a single Indian since we struck the Territory. All that talk about the high-and-mighty Apaches turned out to be bunkum."

"That's right," the older man said. "We were led to believe Apaches lurk behind every bush. But nothing could be further from the truth."

"It only takes one," Fargo said, "and you have five to deal with. Saddle up and we'll light a shuck."

"Not so fast," the younger man responded. "We don't know you from Adam. Yet you expect us to do as you want with no questions asked?"

"I expect you want to live."

Until that moment the portrait of loveliness had been silent. Now she cleared her throat and said softly, almost timidly, "Perhaps we should heed him, Uncle George. He seems most sincere."

"Outlaws and brigands often do, Tricia," George said. "You are too trusting. We must never take anyone out here at their word."

Inwardly, Fargo fumed. If not for the woman he would leave the lunkheads then and there.

"But if there *are* Apaches—" Tricia began, and was given no chance to finish her statement.

"For all we know this fellow is trying to lure us into an ambush," the younger man cut her off. "We were warned that this country is crawling with cutthroats and outlaws, remember?"

"Harold is right," George said. "If we are to reach Paradise Valley, we must keep our wits about us and take every precaution. Whoever this frontiersman is, he doesn't look very trustworthy to me."

Fargo's temper flared. "Mister, you're a jackass, and you're about to get the lady killed. In a couple of minutes the Apaches will be here."

"So you claim," George replied. "I think it best you ride on. If there really are Apaches, now that you have forewarned us, we can fend them off."

Harold nodded. "My father is right. I can drop a squirrel at three hundred yards with this." He wagged the Sharps. "Any Apache that so much as shows an eyeball will be sent to whatever special hell is reserved for heathens."

Fargo lifted his reins and was all set to touch his spurs to the Ovaro when he saw the mute appeal in the young woman's eyes. She knew her uncle and cousin were making a mistake. "Suit yourselves," Fargo said, acting as if

5

he did not care one way or the other what they did. "It's your funeral." He reined the Ovaro around to the south as if he intended to ride on. But no sooner did the stallion take a few steps than he reined it back around, palming the Colt as the Ovaro turned, and thumbed back the hammer.

The ruse worked. Both George and Harold, thinking they had buffaloed him, had started to lower their rifles. Before they could raise them again, they were staring into the business end of Fargo's six-shooter.

"I wouldn't," Fargo said when Harold went to hike the Sharps. He half hoped the man would try anyway, but Harold angrily jerked the Sharps down and scowled.

"I knew it!" George declared. "You are an outlaw! You intend to rob us and leave us for the buzzards!"

"I intend to save your worthless hides," Fargo informed him, "whether you want me to or not." He did not add that he was only doing it for the woman. "Set your rifles down and saddle your horses, and be quick about it."

"Pa?" Harold said, still eager to shoot.

Uncertainty seeped into the older man's features. "We'll do as he wants for now, son. If it is a trick, we will take action when the time is right." George slowly lowered his Ballard rifle to the ground.

Gnawing on his lower lip, Harold hesitated. "I don't like this, Pa. I don't like it one bit."

"Would you like being roasted alive more?" Fargo was about at the end of his patience. "Or maybe staked under the sun, with your eyes gouged out and your tongue cut from your mouth?"

"You're just trying to scare us," Harold said. But he set the Sharps down and turned to the saddles. "I'll do yours, Tricia," he offered, "then mine. You rest easy. I won't let this scoundrel harm you."

Fargo risked a glance up the canyon. As yet there was no sign of the Apaches, but that did not mean anything. They were masters at hiding in plain sight, at blending in so they appeared to be part of the terrain. They could be twenty feet from him and he would not know it until it was too late.

6

A footfall caused Fargo to twist toward the three travelers, but it was only the woman. She had stepped close to the Ováro and was regarding him intently. "Something on your mind?"

"I want to thank you for coming to our aid. Uncle George and Harold mean well, but they tend to be too protective of me."

Fargo could not fault them for that. "They should be. Females are scarce in these parts." Females as attractive as her were even scarcer. "What are you doing here? Bound for Las Cruces?" It made sense. Las Cruces was the next town to the south, a hundred miles or so as the raven flew, across some of the most godforsaken landscape on the continent.

"Oh, no. We're on our way to Paradise Valley."

"Never heard of it," Fargo admitted. Which was not unusual. New settlements sprang up all the time.

"It's southwest of Fort Craig about seventy or eighty miles," Tricia revealed.

Fargo envisioned the entirety of New Mexico Territory in his mind's eye. That would place Paradise Valley somewhere in the Mimbres Mountains, the haunt of the Mimbres Apaches. The tribe was led by the renowned Mangas Colorado, and the list of whites and Mexicans they had slain was longer than all of Fargo's arms and legs combined. He could no more imagine the Mimbres allowing whites to settle on Mimbre land than he could the Mimbres allowing themselves to be herded like sheep onto a reservation, as the government wanted. "There are whites there now?"

"And have been for quite a while," Tricia answered.

That simply could not be, Fargo told himself, but he put the matter aside for the time being and once more scanned the upper reaches of the canyon. Any moment now the canyon walls might resound to the blast of Apache rifles.

Tricia extended her hand. "I'm Patricia Haxton, by the way. Everyone calls me Tricia."

Fargo introduced himself.

"My parents are already at Paradise Valley," she went

on. "I came west with Uncle George and Harold to see them. We have not run into any difficulties until now."

Was it a trick of the sunlight and shadows, or had Fargo glimpsed movement an arrow's flight away? "Hurry it up," he growled at the two men. George was about done but Harold dawdled.

Patricia Haxton was disposed to talk. "What are you doing in New Mexico, Mr. Fargo, if I might ask? Do you live here? Have a wife and children, perhaps?"

"The army wants me to report to Major Marshall at Fort Craig." Fargo had visited many military posts in his wanderings, but not Craig. It had been established seven years ago at the north end of the dreaded Jornada del Muerto to help keep the Mimbres and other tribes in line.

"You are in the army, then?"

Fargo shook his head. "I work for them from time to time, scouting and such." He did not know why his presence had been requested at Fort Craig. Marshall was supposed to tell him when he got there.

"You have had dealings with Apaches before, I take it."

"Once or twice."

"What do you think of them? As a people, I mean. Uncle George is of the opinion that they are little better than animals. He accepts the popular notion that the only good redskin is a dead redskin."

"What about you?" Fargo asked. He was all too aware of the general sentiment. As the newspapers were so fond of stressing, most whites viewed Indians as impediments to westward expansion. What it boiled down to was land. Land the Indians occupied. Land the whites wanted.

"My mother taught me not to judge others, but let their actions speak for them," Tricia said. "Some Indians are nice. Some aren't. They are no different than us in that regard."

Fargo's opinion of her rose several notches.

"I just wish everyone could get along," Tricia said wistfully, "but that's not human nature, is it? There is always someone at someone else's throat. Wars and rumors of war, isn't that how it goes? I suppose it is silly to want the white man and the red man to live in peace, but one can always hope."

Suddenly Fargo stiffened. There could be no mistake. Something had moved among the boulders.

"What is it?" Tricia asked, gazing in the same direction. "What do you see up there?"

Before Fargo could tell her, a swarthy form reared up and took deliberate aim. He fired without thinking, elevating the Colt a fraction to compensate for the distance, and was rewarded with a spark of lead on stone. He had missed, but the Apache ducked down without firing.

Others rose from concealment. Thunder echoed off the canyon walls as Fargo shoved the Colt into its holster. Bending low, he looped his arm around Patricia Haxton's slim waist and swept her up behind him. She cried out in surprise, and then they were past her uncle and her cousin and racing down the canyon, her arms tight around his midriff, her warm cheek against his back between his shoulder blades. "Ride for your lives!" he shouted.

A hasty glance showed George Haxton clambering onto his horse. Harold was frozen in shock. Spumes of dust spurted at his feet, and he awoke to the danger and sprang to his mount. The horse had other ideas, and bolted down the canyon with Patricia's animal close behind.

"Pa!" Harold bawled.

Fargo slowed. He must do what he could. But just then George Haxton imitated his example and leaned down to swing Harold up behind him. The younger Haxton straddled the animal as yet another shot rang out, and Harold reacted as if he had been punched in the spine. The son would have fallen if not for his father, who clamped an arm around him and gave the horse its head.

The five Apaches, realizing their quarry was escaping, burst from concealment and bounded in pursuit. Firing on the run, they sought to bring the horses down before the animals were out of range.

It had long been one of Fargo's secret fears that one day he would lose the Ovaro. That the pinto would step in a prairie dog hole or suffer some other mishap and break a leg, or be stolen, or be shot out from under him, as threatened to be the case now, with slugs buzzing and whining all about. He reined right and then left, zigzagging to make them harder to hit.

Tricia's fingers dug into his ribs. Her excited breaths fluttered at the nape of his neck. But she did not scream in panic or succumb to a fit of hysterics, even when a leaden bee nearly stung the two of them.

A squeal pierced the air. Fargo shifted and beheld the horse that belonged to Harold Paxton tumbling hard to the rocky slope, a red mist gushing from a hole high in its neck. It slid a good ten feet. Then, head and legs thrashing, it tried to stand. It almost made it. But another slug smashed it back down.

George Haxton was bent low. Harold, clutching his back, gazed at the dead horse in outrage as they went by it. Twisting, Harold shook a fist at the pursuing Apaches and shouted something that was drowned out by more shots. The next second, his clenched fist jerked violently and a finger arced toward the sky trailing scarlet drops. Harold howled and nearly fell off. Only his father's restraining arm saved him.

Suddenly a boulder loomed directly in front of the Ovaro. Reining sharply, Fargo avoided it. Tricia had to hold on tighter, and he could feel the contours of her bosom on his back. She was nicely endowed.

The firing dwindled to a few random shots, and ceased. "They've stopped shooting!" Tricia exclaimed the obvious.

Apaches were not ones to waste precious ammunition. The warriors stood staring sullenly after them.

Fargo did not stop until he had covered over a mile. Drawing rein, he grasped Tricia's wrist and swung her down. The instant her feet touched, she ran to meet her uncle and cousin.

Harold had his hand pressed to his homespun shirt. A scarlet stain covered much of the front. His head was thrown back, his teeth gritted in agony. "They shot me!" he wailed. "The filthy vermin shot me!"

Any sympathy Fargo entertained died. He covered them as Tricia and George carefully lowered Harold to the parched ground.

"How bad is it, son?"

Harold held up his hand, and the fingers on that hand, minus one. Blood trickled from the stub. Shoving the stump against his side to staunch the flow, he groaned. "My hand hurts worse than my back."

"It's only one finger," George said. "You can make do with those you have left." He carefully eased his son over so he could examine Harold's back. The slug had dug a deep furrow inches above Harold's belt but had not struck a vital organ. Harold would live.

"You've lost a lot of blood, cousin," Tricia said, "but the bleeding has pretty much stopped."

Harold reached up with his good hand and grabbed his father by the shirt. "I want them dead, Pa. Do you hear me? I want to go back and kill every last one of those red scum."

"That might not be wise, son," George said.

"There are only five of them. We can wait until dark. Take them by surprise." Harold stiffened resentfully when Fargo chuckled.

"Take Apaches by surprise? They can hear better than you, they can see better than you, they can smell better than you, too. They'll know you're coming long before you're close enough to kill them. Forget it."

Harold thrust his bloody hand at Fargo, displaying the stub. "Forget *this*? Forget what they have done to me? Mister, I owe them Apaches, and if it's the last thing I ever do, I will make them pay."

Fargo had heard similar bluster before and gave it no more heed than worthless hot air was due. "Right now we need to think about putting more distance between them and us. We're not safe until we're sure we have shaken them." Fargo was fairly certain the five warriors

11

had not come after them, but then again, Apaches were notoriously unpredictable.

"My son needs rest," George Haxton said.

"He can get all the sleep he wants when we stop for the night," Fargo responded. "We do this my way, or I ride off and leave you. I won't let your stupidity get me killed." Tricia notwithstanding.

George did not hide his disgust. "I don't think I like you very much."

"I do," Patricia said, smiling sweetly. "I like Mr. Fargo a whole lot. Let's do as he wants, and everything will be all right."

"All right?" Fargo grimly shook his head. "Hell, girl. We'll be lucky if we get out of this alive."

2

Harold Haxton would not stop groaning.

Fargo, who was standing guard while the others slept, barely contained his annoyance. Tricia had bandaged her cousin's wounds and done a good job. Granted, they had to hurt, and granted, the loss of a finger was enough to upset anyone, but Harold behaved more like a ten-year-old than a grown man. He had whined and complained the whole rest of the day.

Another groan rose from the sleeping man's throat, and Fargo nearly walked over and kicked him. The groans were not loud, but they were loud enough for roving Apaches to hear and investigate.

A multitude of stars blazed in the New Mexico sky. Coyotes, now and again, gave voice to their sharp cries. From the northwest wafted a strong, welcome breeze. Fargo heard no night birds, which was encouraging. Sometimes they were not birds at all but came from human throats.

It was a perfectly ordinary, perfectly peaceful night, and Fargo would not have it any other way.

George Haxton was on his side under a blanket. Thankfully, he wasn't a snorer. Tricia was a few yards away, her back to them. They had turned in over an hour ago, but Fargo's instincts told him she was not asleep. Although why, when she needed the rest, he could not say. Unless fear had her, too, on edge. Fear of the Apaches and what the Apaches would do to her if they got their hands on her.

13

In one respect Tricia stood to be better off than the rest of them; Apaches sometimes let female captives live, and took them for their own. Often the captives proved too weak for Apache tastes and were slain anyway.

Shifting his Henry from the crook of his left elbow to the crook of his right, Fargo stretched, then resumed pacing in a wide circle. The horses were dozing, which was a good sign. The Ovaro usually warned him when hostiles were about.

Fargo was gazing to the east when he heard the rustle of a blanket and the soft shuffle of feet. He did not turn around to see who it was. He did not need to. "Can't sleep, I take it."

"No," Patricia Haxton said. "I'm too overwrought, what with the Apaches out to kill us."

"They come with the territory," Fargo quipped.

"A territory I did not want to come to. I would as soon be safe and happy back in Indiana. But I could hardly refuse my parents."

Fargo looked at her. She had a shawl wrapped around her slender shoulders, and her hair shone faintly in the starlight. "You're old enough to stand on your own two feet."

"I suppose," Tricia said. "But we are a close-knit family. Or we were. It would never occur to me to refuse my parents' request."

"Even if that request gets you killed?" Fargo was blunt about the plight she had placed herself in. New Mexico was no place for amateurs.

"Through thick and thin, Mr. Fargo," Tricia said a trifle testily. "Or that's how it used to be and how I would like it to be again. Surely you can appreciate a little thing like devotion to one's family."

"I appreciate a lot of things, lady, but not stupidity," Fargo said. The Haxtons were fish out of water. They had no business being there, and he said as much.

"Who are you to judge us?" was Tricia's counter. "And here I took you to be considerate. I see now I was mistaken. You tend to think you are better than everyone else."

"Don't put words in my mouth," Fargo said gruffly. "If you want to be turned into worm food, go right ahead. I learned a long time ago that some people go through life with blinders on, and nothing I say or do will get them to take the blinders off."

Tricia was quiet awhile. The wind swirled her hair across her face but she did not brush it aside. Finally she said softly, "My apologies. I am taking out my unease on you. I plead fatigue." She changed the subject. "We'll reach Fort Craig tomorrow, correct?"

"If all goes well."

"From there it is only several days more to Paradise Valley," Tricia said without much enthusiasm. "I'll finally see my mother and father again. I can hardly wait."

To Fargo she did not sound excited by the prospect. More like she was dreading it. "How many people are at this valley of yours?"

"Sixteen or seventeen families, I believe," Tricia surprised him. "My father mentioned them in one of his letters."

"What are they doing there? Prospecting?" Fargo probed. In recent years gold and silver seekers had ventured into the rugged fastness of Apache country, many never to emerge. Those who did not fall victim to Apaches fell victim to the land.

"Goodness gracious, no," Tricia said, laughing lightly. "My parents are farmers. And all those who have joined my father are tillers of the soil. It is the one requirement he has set down."

"Indiana and Illinois have better farmland," Fargo mentioned. As did just about every state east of the Mississippi River. To come all this way to farm struck him as idiotic.

"But land in Indiana costs money," Tricia said. "Here it is free for the taking."

"Because no one else wants it, except the Apaches," Fargo noted. And a few other tribes he could think of.

"They can't keep it to themselves forever. Sooner or later they will be forced to yield. Or haven't you heard of Manifest Destiny?"

Fargo smothered a scowl. Yes, he was all too aware of the prevailing belief that whites had the right to every square foot of land between the Atlantic Ocean and the Pacific. Since some of that land was in the hands of Indians, the Indians had to go, either by being exterminated or forced onto reservations.

"There will come a day when New Mexico Territory is no different than Indiana or Florida or Missouri," Tricia predicted. "When all the Indians have been subdued and we are free to live in peace and prosperity."

"You sound like a damned politician."

"Well, it's true. You can't deny popular sentiment." Tricia endeared herself by adding, "Not that I necessarily agree. Indians are human beings, too, but I'll never get my father or Uncle George to see that."

They were quiet again, until Patricia coughed and shifted her feet and asked, almost timidly, "Is it really as bad as you let on? How many Apaches are there, anyway?"

"East of here are the Mescaleros. To the northeast, the Jicarillas. To the southwest, where you're headed, are the Mimbres. West of them are the Chiricahuas. Then there are the White Mountain Apaches, the Tontos, the Cibecues—"

"Land sakes!" Tricia interrupted. "To listen to you, a body would think the countryside is overrun."

"I haven't even mentioned the other tribes," Fargo said. "The Navajos and those like them who act up from time to time." He gestured, encompassing the vast, benighted wilderness. "Farmers don't belong here. Apaches do."

"But some Indians farm, do they not?"

About to reply, Fargo stiffened. From off in the darkness came a faint rattling sound, like a pebble clattering on rocks. Throwing an arm around Tricia's shoulders, he squatted, pulling her down with him.

"What was that?" she whispered.

"It could be anything," Fargo said, "including Apaches."

"But someone told me Indians don't go around much at night."

"Hush," Fargo said. Thankfully, Harold had temporarily stopped groaning, and in the silence he strained his ears for telltale clues. Tricia was right in that, generally, Indians did not roam around a lot in the dark, but that did not mean they never did, and Apaches were more prone than most tribes to do so.

Another stone rattled, closer this time.

"Stay put," Fargo whispered, and started to move in the direction the sounds came from. But he had only taken a few steps when her fingers closed on his forearm, stopping him short.

"Don't leave us."

"I have to," Fargo whispered. It was wiser to take the fight to the Apaches than wait for the Apaches to come to them. "Wake up your uncle, but don't make any noise. The two of you keep watch until I get back."

Tricia's lovely eyes were pools of anxiety. "What if you don't?"

"Then saddle the horses and light a shuck," Fargo advised. "Ride like hell for Fort Craig."

"We can't desert you," Tricia whispered. "It wouldn't be right."

"Being right doesn't count for much if you're dead," Fargo rebutted. He tugged, and she reluctantly let go. Holding the Henry in front of him, he crept into the gloom. He did not glance back to see if she had obeyed. If she didn't, the consequences were on her head, not his.

He went some forty yards. Leaning his elbows on a waist-high boulder, Fargo wedged the Henry to his shoulder. The Apaches were not likely to show themselves until the very last instant, but he might get off a couple of shots. Then the rest would be on him, and that, as they say, would be that.

Something crunched. A vague silhouette materialized, moving slowly toward him. Puzzlement set in. The figure was upright, not low to the ground as an Apache would be. Fargo could not be sure, but whoever it was seemed to be weaving, as if drunk or hurt. The closer the figure came, the more convinced he became that it was not an Apache.

The figure tripped, either over its own feet or some-thing else, and a curse proved Fargo right. But he was taking no chances. "Hold it right there," he quietly com-manded. Quiet, in case there were others.

Halting, the figure stabbed a hand to its waist.

"I wouldn't," Fargo warned. "I can drop you in your tracks."

"Who's that?" came a nervous retort. "Are you white?"

"Don't I sound it?" Fargo retorted.

"Some Apaches speak English," the man said, "and speak it well. So do bandits from south of the border."

"If I were either you would be dead by now." Fargo thought he saw the glint of buttons and the outline of chevrons on a sleeve. "You're a soldier?"

"Sergeant Tim Francis," the man said. "Look, mister. I'm about done in, and I might have Mimbres on my tail. Do you want me to stand here waiting for a bullet or an arrow in the back, or can we talk?"

"Come ahead, but do it nice and slow and keep your hands where I can see them." Fargo stayed behind the boulder on the off chance it was a trick. Apaches and bandits sometimes helped themselves to the uniforms of slain troopers, and as the man had mentioned, were flu-ent in English.

His arms out from his sides, the man shuffled nearer. He was indeed wearing a uniform, but his hat was miss-ing. Of stocky build, he had thick shoulders and short arms and legs. A square face weathered by exposure to the sun and seamed by the hardship of army life smiled as Fargo stood. "You are white! I don't mind telling you, mister, that I'm about done in."

Fargo looked past him. "You're alone?" He assumed the soldier was part of a patrol that had run into trouble. Troopers never went anywhere by their lonesomes, with one exception.

"I'm a dispatch rider," Sergeant Francis disclosed. "I was on my way from Fort Craig to Fort Marcy with an important dispatch for Colonel Arnold. Five miles out of Craig some Mimbres jumped me. They shot my horse out from under me and I lit out on foot."

"Why didn't you head back to Fort Craig?" Fargo wondered, since the trooper was traveling in the opposite direction.

"Do you think I didn't try? Those red devils were expecting me to, and cut me off. They have been after me ever since. I've swapped shots a few times, but all I have is my revolver." Sergeant Francis patted the flap on his holster. "I lost my carbine when my horse went down. No food, no water, either." He mopped a sleeve across his brow. "I never expected to come on anyone else out here."

"How far back are the Mimbres? Or did you shake them?"

"Shake Apaches?" Sergeant Francis snorted. "That will be the day. No, if I had to guess, I'd say they can't be more than half a mile behind me, if that much. They could come along anytime now. They don't seem to be in any hurry to kill me, though. It's almost as if they're playing cat and mouse."

It sounded like something Apaches would do. "They want to wear you out," Fargo guessed. "Wear you down until you collapse and you're too weak to lift a finger. Then they'll take you prisoner and test your courage."

"By torturing me, you mean, to see how long I'll last." The sergeant's tone was bitter. "I know all about Apache hijinks, mister. When I volunteered to ride dispatch, my friends all said I was as good as dead."

"Then why did you?"

Sergeant Francis shrugged. "Someone has to, and I'm about the best rider at Fort Craig. I've been riding since I was old enough to sit a horse." Francis was stating facts, not bragging. "Besides, most of our men are raw recruits. They can't ride worth a damn and their shooting is worse. Fact is, they can't do much of anything except complain about the heat and the food and the dust."

"Are you hungry?" Fargo asked. "I have some pemmican in my saddlebags and a little water left in my water skin."

"Mister, I would kill for a bite to eat, but filling my belly has to wait until after we've dealt with the Mim-

19

bres." Lifting the flap, Francis drew his revolver. "I only have eleven cartridges left, so every shot has to count."

Fargo was about to say he might have some ammunition he could spare, provided his Colt was the same caliber, when a bird warbled. A bird that was not a bird.

Instantly, Sergeant Francis sprang to a nearby boulder and dropped to his knees. "I told you!" he whispered.

A dilemma confronted Fargo. He needed to warn the Haxtons. But that would take precious seconds he could ill spare. The issue was taken out of his hands by the abrupt appearance of a darkling silhouette that flowed toward them like an unearthly specter. Another appeared, and a third.

The foremost Mimbre was bent low, his forehead nearly scraping the ground. The other two flanked him.

Fargo waited. He wanted them close, so close he could not possibly miss. There was a danger in that, if he missed their vitals by even an inch, they would be on him before he could shoot them again. And wounded Apaches were like wounded bears or wounded mountain lions—twice as fierce, and twice as formidable. He sighted down his Henry at the tracker and fixed the sights on the warrior's sternum. A shot there should rupture the heart.

The Apaches slowed. The tracker placed a hand on the ground. They were at the spot where the soldier had stopped when Fargo made his presence known. He held his fire. They were not quite close enough.

Unexpectedly, Sergeant Francis roared, "Take this, damn you!" and fired. The tracker went down but did not stay down. In the blink of an eye, he sprang back up and all three bounded toward the boulder screening Francis.

Anger washed over Fargo. The soldier had blundered. But he had more important considerations. He fired, and an Apache went over backward in a somersault. He trained the Henry on another Mimbre, but the remaining pair disappeared as if the earth had yawned wide and swallowed them whole. One moment they were there, the next they weren't.

"We got one!" Sergeant Francis whooped.

Fargo did not share the soldier's elation. They had lost the advantage of surprise, and there were still two Mimbres to account for.

"Where did the other two get to?" Francis whispered. "I don't see them anywhere, do you?"

Fargo did not reply. It was ridiculous, after the shouting Francis had just done, to speak softly now. The Mimbres knew where they were. Tense seconds dragged like millstones. Beads of sweat sprinkled Fargo's brow, and he found himself breathing shallowly. Every nerve tingled. At any second, sinewy death might spring at him, or a leaden hornet might inflict a lethal sting.

"Where the blazes are they?" Sergeant Francis anxiously whispered. "What are they waiting for?"

Fargo thought it should be obvious. Apaches weren't fools. The Mimbres would not show themselves again. The warriors would circle around, probably one to either side. He shifted to scan the murk to his rear.

From out of it came an urgent query. "Fargo? Where are you?" George Haxton shouted.

Patricia was with him. "What is happening?" she called out.

"Damn!" Fargo broke from cover, yelling over his shoulder, "Follow me!" He did not look to see if Francis did. It was the woman he was concerned about. She was a prize the Mimbres would not pass up. He willed his legs to fly.

A sharp outcry was borne on the wind. Then lusty oaths punctuated by the *crack* of a rifle. A scream was torn from a female throat, followed by more oaths, and George Haxton bellowing, "Stop! Let go of her, you filthy redskin!"

Fargo glimpsed the uncle's inky silhouette, moving rapidly away, in pursuit of the warriors who had taken Tricia. A body appeared, sprawled in a grotesque contortion brought on by violent death. Harold Haxton's missing finger was no longer of any consequence; he had been shot in the forehead and the slug had ruptured out the crown of his skull.

Without slowing, Fargo vaulted over the prone form and plunged after Uncle George. He could only hope the older Haxton was still after the Apaches and not running aimlessly.

As if to soothe Fargo's worry, a rifle boomed, and was answered. The flash of gunfire spiking the dark drew him like a moth to a flame. He did not shoot because he could not be sure who was who. Then another body hove out of the earth. This time it was George.

The father had shared the son's fate. Only instead of having his brains blown out, George Haxton had been shot in the left cheek and, for good measure, had his throat slit from ear to ear. His eyes were wide in shock and his lips were moving. From his throat came a wet gurgling as deep, rich scarlet flowed from the cut. He saw Fargo, and with a grunt and a mighty effort, rose onto his elbows. Again he tried to say something. Pink froth bubbled from his mouth. Then, with a tiny gasp, he succumbed.

Fargo did not linger. As fleet as a deer, he hurtled in the direction George Haxton had been going. He saw no sign of the Mimbres. He covered twenty yards. Fifty yards. He was about convinced he should stop and listen, and pray he heard some sound that would show where they were.

Almost immediately, a screech rent the wilderness. It was smothered, no doubt by a rough hand over Patricia's mouth, but not entirely. She continued to shriek, a beacon for Fargo's racing feet.

He spotted them.

A burly Mimbre, one brawny arm hooked around Tricia's waist, had his other hand over her mouth. She was resisting tooth and nail by biting at the Apache's fingers and kicking and punching. That she did not break free was not due to a lack of trying. A lesser man would be hard pressed to hold on to her.

But Apaches had a justly deserved reputation for being as hard as the land that bred them. The iron men, they were called, and they lived up to their reputations. They could travel farther in one day than most whites could travel in three, and they could do it on foot, not on horseback. They could go without water and food longer than anyone else. They endured hardships without complaint, and absorbed punishment like a sponge absorbed water. Even more telling, they would rather have their tongues torn out than betray another Apache.

All this went through Fargo's mind as he narrowed the gap. He was so preoccupied that he failed to recollect there were two Mimbres left until a breechclout-clad battering ram slammed into him from the side and he was smashed to the earth like a child in the grip of a giant. Steel glinted, and Fargo jerked his head and neck to one side. The blade bit into the dirt by his ear.

The Apache raised the knife again. If he had used it that instant, he might have prevailed. But Apaches, for all their prowess, were as human as the whites they hated, and not above gloating when they had an enemy at their mercy. The warrior straddling Fargo grinned in triumph and declared, *"Dee-dah tatsan."* Which was Mimbre for, "You will soon be dead."

In the brief seconds it took the Mimbre to gloat, Fargo's right hand closed on his Colt. Jerking the revolver out, he jammed the muzzle against the Apache's barrel chest and fired. At the first shot the Apache jerked. At the second the Apache snarled. At the third a look of amazement came over the Mimbre and he oozed off Fargo in a limp heap.

Fargo levered up onto a knee.

"Skye! Look out!"

Why the last Mimbre did not shoot him, Fargo would never know. Maybe the warrior was so incensed at the sight of Fargo shooting his companion that he wanted to kill Fargo man-to-man. Maybe the last warrior wanted Fargo to suffer before he died, and the rifle would be too quick. Whatever the reason, as Fargo pivoted the Mimbre barreled into him like a swarthy bolt out of the ether, bowling him over with such force that Fargo's breath whooshed from his lungs and excruciating pain racked his ribs.

Fargo twisted as he went down. Once again, he was

on the bottom. Once again, an Apache straddled him. He caught a wrist with his left hand and stopped the descending knife barely an inch from his jugular.

The Apache hissed through clenched teeth and grabbed at Fargo's right wrist to keep him from using the Colt. But the warrior missed his hold. In the next heartbeat, Fargo gouged the Colt's barrel into the triangle of the Mimbre's lower jaw. The hammer was already cocked. All he had to do was squeeze the trigger.

Gasping for breath, sore and battered, Fargo pushed the heavy body off. He slowly rose, his limbs weak from the exertion. He nearly fell when Patricia Haxton threw herself at him and sobbed into his chest.

"Oh God! Oh God! Oh God!"

"Welcome to New Mexico," Skye Fargo said.

3

Shallow graves were better than no graves, and shallow graves were the best Fargo could do. The ground was hard and rocky, and he had nothing to dig with other than a few jagged rocks and his Arkansas toothpick, and he was not about to blunt the knife. Sergeant Francis helped, although he was so worn out that he frequently had to stop to rest.

Patricia Haxton watched sorrowfully as her uncle and cousin were lowered into the holes, tears streaming down her cheeks.

Fargo and the sergeant covered the uncle first. They were about done covering Harold when Tricia cleared her throat. "We should say some words over them. It's proper to do."

"Don't look at me," Sergeant Francis said. "I haven't been to church in a coon's age. I wouldn't know how to go about it."

Tricia looked at Fargo. "What about you? A few words would suffice. Something from Scripture."

"They were your kin," Fargo said. "You do the honors."

"Very well. But I don't attend church much myself since my marriage fell apart," Tricia said a trifle resentfully.

Sergeant Francis shrugged. "I'm no parson, lady, but I doubt it makes much difference to the Almighty. Dead is dead."

So it fell on Tricia, who recited the Twenty-third Psalm

by rote. When she finished, she sprinkled handfuls of dirt on each grave, saying softly, "I will miss both of you dearly. You did not look down your noses at me like some of the others did. You stood by me through thick and thin."

Fargo wondered about her remarks.

She had more. "I pray God will look after your souls, and that you are happier in the hereafter than I have ever been in this life."

They spent the rest of the night in a dry wash. Fargo used picket pins to make it harder for the Mimbres to steal the horses, then hunkered with his arms around his legs and his chin on his knees. He did not use his blanket. It was not cold enough to need one.

Tricia felt differently. She bundled herself so that only her face was showing, and stared off into space, lost in thought until she gave a slight shiver and commented, "I wish we could have a fire."

"Those Apaches might have friends nearby." For Fargo, survival always came before comfort. "Morning will be here before you know it. You'll be plenty warm once the sun is up."

Sergeant Francis was curled on his side. Exhaustion had claimed him, and he was almost asleep. "The damned Mimbres are everywhere," he said drowsily. "They've been stirred up like riled wasps."

"By what?" Fargo asked. Not that Apaches ever needed an excuse to go on the warpath.

"By some damned stupid settlers," Francis answered. "Jackasses who went and helped themselves to land in the heart of Mimbre territory."

"Those settlers you mentioned are relatives and friends of mine," Tricia said. "I know for a fact the land they have settled on is land to which the Apaches have no legal claim."

Sergeant Francis roused and rose on an elbow. "Lady, the Mimbres roamed these parts long before we came along. I'm no Indian lover, but they were here first, and that makes the land theirs as far as they're concerned."

"They should have filed on it," Tricia said defensively.

"What do Apaches know of land rights and claims? You sound like that damn fool leader out at Paradise Valley."

"That fool is my father."

"Oh." Francis muttered something and sank back down, pulling the blanket Fargo had lent him up over his head. "Your pa isn't exactly the most popular gent in New Mexico right at the moment. He's caused a lot of bloodshed. The Mimbres were bad enough before he came. Now they're roaming the countryside and killing every white they come across."

"You can't blame him," Tricia said defensively.

"Like hell we can't. My commanding officer, Major Marshall, sent me to Fort Marcy for help. I'll have to try again after we get to Fort Craig. If I don't make it, my life will be one of the many on your father's shoulders."

"That's absurd," Tricia said. The sergeant did not reply, and in due course light snores came from under the blanket. "You don't believe him, do you?" she asked Fargo. "About my father, I mean."

"The Mimbres don't like settlers."

"But that's unfair to my father," Tricia complained. "This land is free for the taking. How can the army hold it against civilians who want to make new lives for themselves? The government should be grateful there are people willing to brave the dangers." She paused, then ruefully grinned. "Listen to me. I do sound just like my father. And I was the one who spoke out against the idea back in Ohio."

"Then why are you here?" Fargo asked.

"Things didn't work out for me. But that's life, isn't it? We can't ever predict how it will turn out."

"It would be boring if we could." Fargo always preferred the unknown to the known. He always had to see what lay over the next horizon. It was part of the reason men had taken to calling him the Trailsman.

"Maybe so," Tricia said. "But it's my own fault. I took someone for granted and I shouldn't have."

"A lover?"

Tricia's chin jutted at him like an accusing finger. "Really, now. Whatever gave you that idea?"

Fargo merely smiled. He had learned to read people almost as well as he read tracks.

"Although I am sorry to admit you are closer to the truth than you realize. I married a man my parents did not want me to marry. They warned me he was worthless and shiftless, but I was too much in love to listen."

"They were right, I take it."

"He left me. Just up and took off without a note or a good-bye or anything. I couldn't believe it. I thought he cared for me as much as I cared for him. He broke my heart and made me out to be a fool in the bargain."

"It's not foolish to fall in love," Fargo remarked.

Tricia brightened. "What a nice thing to say. But my parents felt differently. They said I was too young. That I was taken by how handsome he was, but that handsome is only skin deep. My mother begged me not to marry him and my father threatened to never talk to me again, but I did it anyway." She sighed, and frowned. "I thought I knew better than they did. I was wrong."

"Do they know you are coming?"

"No. I thought I would surprise them. Uncle George came down here with my father, but had to return to Ohio to sign some papers dealing with the sale of his farm. I pleaded with him to bring me and he gave in." Her voice broke, and Tricia gazed toward the graves. "Uncle George always treated me so nice. He never had a daughter, but always wanted one."

Fargo listened to the wind, and for sounds the wind might carry with it, but the night was deceptively tranquil. "Maybe you should think about going back."

"To Ohio? After coming all this way? After Uncle George and Harold gave their lives protecting me?"

"You could end up just like them."

"It would serve me right," Tricia said. "Maybe it's what I deserve for being so pigheaded."

Fargo did not say anything. He was not one to judge others. She must deal with her guilt on her own. He settled back, making himself comfortable. The sun would not rise for four hours. Hours he would dearly like to use to sleep. He was bone tired. But one of them had to stay awake and alert.

Time passed. Fargo took it for granted that Tricia had dozed off and was surprised when she stirred and asked a question. "Are you married?"

"No."

"A handsome man like you?" She sounded skeptical. "How can that be? I'd imagine you have to beat women off with a stick."

"Shouldn't you be sleeping?" The last thing Fargo was willing to discuss was females.

"I can't sleep. I'm too worked up over Uncle George and Harold. I loved them dearly."

"It will be a long, hard ride to Fort Craig," Fargo said. He did not add that the Mimbres might pounce at any time.

"Don't fret on my account. I'll keep up. I promise," Tricia vowed. "I was a bit of a tomboy growing up. My folks tried their utmost to turn me into a lady, but I've always had an independent streak."

Since she would not heed his advice, Fargo made small talk. "Will they be happy to see you?"

"I doubt it. My father thinks I'm a harlot for marrying against his wishes, and my mother always abides by his decisions. He made it plain he never wanted to set eyes on me again."

"Yet here you are." Fargo idly glanced toward the horses and saw that the Ovaro had its head up.

"I had nowhere else to go. I couldn't make do on my own. The job I had as a seamstress didn't pay enough."

Fargo tensed. The Ovaro had pricked its ears. Something was out there, but was it an animal—or Apaches?

"I'll throw myself at their mercy," Tricia was saying. "Maybe my father will relent for once. He's always going on about how we should forgive and forget, but he's the least forgiving man I know. Lest you think ill of me, I have always tried to do as they wanted. Pretty much, anyway," she added, and grinned.

Sergeant Francis had stopped snoring and the wind

had died. Otherwise Fargo would not have heard the faint suggestion of *something* that brought him up off the ground and over to Patricia Haxton. Placing a hand over her mouth, he whispered in her ear, "Not a peep. We might have visitors."

The whites of her eyes grew larger, and she nodded.

Hunched low, Fargo crept up the side of the wash. He removed his hat and flattened. He expected Tricia to stay where she was, but he had not expressly forbidden her to move, and a second later she was beside him, the rustle of her dress much too loud for his liking. Grabbing her arm, he was about to whisper for her to go back down when a low, guttural voice came out of the darkness.

Figures appeared. Not one or two or three but a lot of figures, fifteen or more. Fargo did not need to see them clearly to know they were Mimbres.

Tricia's hand closed on his in stark fear.

The Apaches came nearer. They were moving in single file except for two in the lead, who were whispering and gesturing, apparently in disagreement. When they were ten feet from the dry wash, they suddenly stopped and the two leaders began arguing heatedly.

The war party bristled with weapons. All it would take was the slightest of sounds from the horses or Sergeant Francis, and Fargo would be up to his neck in Apaches.

One of the leaders pointed west. The other pointed north. They were disagreeing over which way to go.

Fargo glanced at the horses. The Ovaro was stock-still. The other horse was sleeping, which was just as well. It might be tempted to whinny.

Tricia's grip on Fargo's hand became an iron vise. The reason had to do with a swarthy warrior who was walking toward them.

Prepared to make his life cost the Apaches dearly, Fargo went to raise the Henry. But the warrior was looking at the ground, not at them, and picked that moment to stop and hitch at his breechclout.

Tricia tried to pull free so she could slide to the bottom of the wash. When Fargo did not let go, she glared.

Suddenly the other horse stirred.

Fargo held his breath. He could count on the Ovaro not to make a sound, but the Haxton's animal was as blind to the dangers of the frontier as its former owners had been.

The Apache was done. The others were waiting for him. The leaders had stopped arguing and were facing west, and as soon as he rejoined them, the war party loped off at a dogtrot.

Quickly, Fargo let go of Tricia and leaped to the bottom of the wash. He ran to the Haxtons' bay and placed his hand on its muzzle, forestalling a neigh. He watched Tricia, who had stayed where she was and was watching the departing Mimbres. Presently she rose and, staying bent over, came down the slope to his side. "They're gone. For the time being, we are safe."

"Don't kid yourself," Fargo said. They would not be safe until they reached Fort Craig

At that juncture, Sergeant Francis mumbled in his sleep, turned onto his back, and commenced snoring.

Tricia giggled. "Thank goodness he didn't do that while those awful Apaches were up there." She cocked her head toward Fargo. "You know, it occurs to me that I haven't thanked you for all you have done."

"No need."

"Sure there is." Tricia kissed him on the cheek. Not a chaste peck, but a lingering kiss that impressed the full, moist feel of her lips on his skin. "That's for saving us the first time. This is for saving me from those two who carried me off." She kissed him again, on the mouth, and her bosom brushed his chest.

On an impulse, Fargo parted his lips and ran the tip of his tongue over her upper lip. To his delight, her mouth opened and her tongue met his in a silken swirl. She tasted of coffee and salt, and more. He let her decide when to break the kiss.

"Oh, my!" Tricia fanned her face with her hand. "I hope you won't think it bold of me to say you strike my fancy."

Fargo was beginning to understand why her father was

so mad at her. "Remind me of that again when we get to the fort."

"It's been months," Tricia said, and when he arched an eyebrow, she explained. "Months since my husband walked out on me. He left shortly after my folks headed for New Mexico Territory. Almost as if he was waiting for them to go so they wouldn't try to stop him."

"You should get some sleep," Fargo repeated his earlier suggestion.

"But I'm not even a little bit sleepy. Blame those Apaches. You should have heard my heart pound when that one came toward us." Tricia smiled suggestively. "I have an idea. How about if we take a stroll."

"You're loco."

"Walking will help quiet my nerves." Tricia playfully pulled on his hand. "Come on. What harm can it do with the Apaches gone?"

"We don't know as they are." But Fargo went anyway, permitting her to lead him east until they had gone a dozen yards and were well out of sight and hearing of Sergeant Francis. "This is far enough."

"It wasn't much of a stroll." Tricia clasped her hands behind her back and tilted her body to admire the stars. In doing so, her breasts thrust against her dress, accenting their swell. "It's pretty here at night, isn't it?"

Fargo chuckled.

Tricia turned and innocently asked, "What's so funny?" In the starlight, her full lips were begging to be tasted, her breasts were twin melons, eager to be fondled. "In case you haven't noticed, I'm female. I like pretty night skies."

"In case you haven't noticed," Fargo mimicked her, "I'm male. I like things like pretty females." So saying, he leaned the Henry against a boulder, straightened, and cupped her breasts. She gasped, more in delight than shock, and gasped again when he pinched both her nipples between his thumbs and forefingers. Lowering his hands, he said, "Is that what you wanted?"

"Must you be so crude? That's not the sort of question a gentleman asks a lady."

"I'm no gentleman."

"And I'm no lady? Is that what you are implying?" Her feelings were hurt, and it showed.

"There you go again. Putting words in my mouth." Fargo hated it when women did that, and they did it all the time.

"Then what are you saying?" Tricia demanded.

"That I like your body," Fargo said, wrapping his right arm around her slim hips and molding her body to his.

"But what about me? Don't you like me as a person? There's more to a woman than her physical charms."

Fargo dipped his mouth to her neck and licked the pale softness of her throat. She trembled slightly, and her hands rose to push against his chest.

"I'm having second thoughts. Maybe you're not the man I thought you were. I want to go back."

"Are you sure?" Fargo asked, and slid his left hand between her legs. The smooth cotton of her dress grew warm to his caress, and she threw back her head and grimaced as if she were in pain.

"Damn you," she husked. "You don't leave a girl her illusions."

"There you go again," Fargo chided, "thinking you can think like me. Take me as I am or don't take me at all."

"But we've only just met." Tricia locked eyes with him. "All I really know is that you are about the most handsome man I have ever met, and when I look at you, I want to do things I haven't done since my good-for-nothing husband walked out on me."

"What's stopping you?" Fargo covered her mouth with his. For a few fleeting seconds she did not react but stood as still as a statue, except for the fluttering of her warm breath. Then she melted into his embrace and cooed softly, deep in her throat. They shared a kiss that went on and on. Parting at last, Fargo put his hand on her breast and kneaded it.

Tricia was panting. "My folks would have a fit if they could see us now."

"You're old enough to live life how you want to live

33

it." Fargo tucked at the knees, and slid his hand as low as he could go in order to locate the hem of her dress.

"Try telling that to my father and mother. To them I will always be their little girl."

"Enough about them." Fargo kissed her again to silence her, while simultaneously delving up under her homespun. His palm caressed the sweet velvet sheen of skin from her knee to high along her inner thigh.

Tricia pulled back but held tight to his biceps. "Mercy me, you work fast. You don't let a girl catch her breath."

"Not when there are Apaches about, no," Fargo said. She wanted it, and he was more than willing to oblige, but they did not have the luxury of taking their time. "If you object, now is when you say so."

"You don't beat around the bush, either," Tricia said with a wry grin. "Do you reckon it's safe enough?"

"*Now* you think of that?" Fargo snorted in amusement. For all their talk about men only having one thing on their minds, women were no different. They pretended to be, but they had the same needs men did, the same desires.

"There you go again. Poking fun at me."

"Speaking of poking—" Fargo said, and with a deft twist and sweep of his forearm, he flicked his fingers up her underthings to her nether lips. They were warm and moist to the touch.

"Oh God!" Tricia arched her back, her mouth agape, her body poised for either pleasure or flight. It was hard to say which until she put her hands on either side of his head and pulled his face down to hers. "Kiss me, damn you. Kiss me and make me forget, if only for a while."

"I never refuse a lady." Fargo smirked. He fused their mouths, and at the same time lightly rubbed the tip of his forefinger across her tiny knob. It was the trigger that transformed her into an inferno of raw passion. She clung to him, one leg curled around his, her hands exploring everywhere, her mouth conveying the sensual depths of her need.

Fargo had to forgo shedding clothes. The Apaches

were out there, somewhere, and it would not do to have the Mimbres stumble on them stark naked. Prying at his belt buckle, he freed his burgeoning manhood. Then, his right arm under her bottom, he lifted Tricia bodily off the ground, positioned her just right, and thrust up into her, impaling her to the quick.

"Ohhhhhhhhh!"

"Not another sound or we stop right now," Fargo told her. She nodded and bit her lip. Holding on to her hips, he drew his pole almost out, then lanced up into her again.

Whimpering, Tricia placed her forehead on his shoulder. "You have no idea what you do to me." She breathed.

"Care to bet?" Fargo adopted a rhythm of almost out and in, almost out and in. Her inner walls sheathed him like a glove, and she met each of his upward thrusts with a downward thrust of her own. They gradually moved faster, ever faster, until it strained his legs to stay on his feet.

"Yes!" Tricia whispered. "I am almost there!"

So was Fargo. He bit her neck. He nipped an earlobe. He tweaked one nipple and then the other. He eased a hand under her dress and touched her. Suddenly she bucked like a wild mare and was over the brink. She gushed and gushed. Her release triggered his.

Afterward, Tricia leaned against him, breathless and flushed. She twined her fingers in his hair, and snickered. "I must say, it has been a pleasure to make your acquaintance."

Fargo grinned.

The next instant their lighthearted mood was shattered by a piercing scream.

4

The scream seemed to go on forever. It came from the west—not close, but not far. Rising to the highest pitch a human voice could reach, it abruptly ended in a terrified bleat. Then the night was quiet again.

Fargo had his clothes as they should be and the Henry in his hands before the cry died. Tricia was rigid with bewilderment. Nudging her, he whispered, "Pull yourself together."

"Was that the sergeant, do you think?"

"I doubt it," Fargo said. It was the wrong direction, for one thing, and it was unlikely Francis had strayed from their camp.

As soon as Tricia was ready, Fargo took her hand and ran. They rounded a bend in the wash and there were the horses, their ears pricked. He did not see Francis anywhere.

"Oh, no! It was him, after all."

Sergeant Francis picked that instant to step from behind the horses. "There you are! Where in hell did you get to? A scream woke me. I thought for sure you had gone off and gotten yourselves killed."

"Keep your voice down," Fargo cautioned. "A war party went past while you were sleeping."

Francis started, and glanced right and left in alarm. "Why didn't you wake me?" he demanded.

"They were too close."

"So you left me lying here as helpless as a newborn babe. Is that it?" Sergeant Francis demanded.

Tricia came to Fargo's defense. "Don't be silly. We were up the wash when we saw them, and heard the same scream you did."

The sergeant's anger faded. He muttered a few words, then groused, "I still don't like being left alone. Those red devils are ghosts. They sneak up on you and it's over before you can blink. Unless they want to have their idea of fun first." He shuddered.

"What do we do now?" Tricia asked.

"We head for the fort. What else?" Sergeant Francis said. "I'll ride double with one of you."

"And be caught in the open?" Fargo shook his head. "It's better to stay put until daybreak."

"Do you see this uniform?" Francis responded. "It means I'm in charge, and we do as I want."

"Do you see this?" Fargo hefted the Henry. "It means I'm not going to let you get us killed."

Sergeant Francis took a step toward him, but all he did was glower. Lowering his revolver, he said sullenly, "I suppose you're right. The smart thing is to stay low. But it's hell on the nerves."

"You, too?" Tricia said.

Fargo offered to keep watch. Tricia and the sergeant lay down, but tossed and fidgeted and eventually gave up. Hour after uneventful hour went by. Toward dawn Fargo handed out pieces of pemmican. By the time a pink blush heralded the new day, they were anxious to be on their way.

As Fargo was tightening the cinch on the Ovaro's saddle, a shadow attached itself to his elbow.

"I don't want to hurt the sergeant's feelings, but I would rather ride double with you than with him. Do you mind?"

"Can you behave yourself?"

Tricia laughed, then pretended to pout. "If you insist. Just don't blame me if I become frisky. There is something about you that brings out a woman's innermost desires."

"That explains a lot." Fargo grinned.

Before the sun rose, they were under way. Sergeant

Francis offered to take the lead, saying he was familiar with the country and could guide them to the fort by the shortest route. Fargo let him, even though he was capable of doing it just as well, if not better. They held to a walk to spare their mounts. By ten o'clock the temperature was over ninety degrees, by Fargo's reckoning. By noon it was pushing one hundred.

"This place is an oven." Tricia had her arms loosely looped around his waist and her cheek on his shoulder. "I'm being baked alive."

"Summer doesn't last forever," Fargo reminded her.

"You don't seem to be affected all that much." Tricia ran a sleeve across her perspiring face. "How do you stand it? If I had known New Mexico was like this, I never would have come."

"You get used to it," Fargo said. Years of living in the wild had lent him the endurance of an Apache. Heat that could fry a man's brain, cold that could freeze blood in its veins; nature's severest extremes had tempered him as a blacksmith tempered steel.

"If you say so." Tricia was skeptical. "But after what those Mimbres did to Uncle George and Harold, I doubt I'll stay long."

"You're scared of the Apaches?"

"What sort of question is that? Of course I am. Any sane person would be. I have no wish to die, thank you very much." Tricia squinted across the baked landscape. "My father made New Mexico sound like a land of milk and honey. But it's hell on earth, and overrun by demons."

"Indians are people, remember?" Fargo said.

"Other tribes, maybe. Tribes like the Shoshones. I've read about them. They live in quaint lodges made of buffalo hides. The men hunt. The women sew and cook. They're not much different than us." Tricia paused. "Apaches are not like the Shoshones. Apaches live to kill, to raid, to plunder. I was told that they were terrible but I didn't believe it. Now I do, and it's only common sense that as soon as I have seen my mother and father, I leave New Mexico Territory and never, ever return. I refuse to end up like my uncle and cousin. I am young yet. I have a lot of living to do."

Fargo did not begrudge her wish to live to old age. In his case it was pointless to harbor the same wish, because it was unlikely he would live past forty. His life was too violent. Somewhere out there was an arrow or a bullet with his name carved into it, or fangs and claws that would end his wanderlust permanently. Until then, he would live each day as it came and do his best to stay alive to greet the next dawn.

About the middle of the afternoon, a dust cloud rose to the northwest. They immediately sought cover in an arroyo. From its rim they spied half a dozen swarthy warriors on horseback, heading east.

"The country is crawling with them," Sergeant Francis muttercd. "And all because your father helped himself to land the Mimbres claim as theirs. I hope it makes you proud, Miss Haxton."

"You have a vulgar mind," Tricia chided.

"Because I think your father is as dumb as a stump and a bastard to boot?" Francis snorted. "Lady, you'll find out soon enough that most whites in these parts think the same as I do. If a vote were held tomorrow, your father would win the most-hated-hombre-in-the-territory award."

"The Apaches have been killing for years. You can't blame this latest outbreak on him."

"Sure I can. Ever heard the two rules, you might call them, that the Apaches live by? To kill without being killed, and to steal without being caught. That's their whole life in a walnut shell."

"So?"

"So your father has given them an excuse to kill like they have never killed before. They hate him and what he's done, and other whites are suffering on his account."

"I just don't understand," Tricia said sadly. "What was my father thinking, coming here? Didn't he realize how the Apaches would feel?"

"The major has been wondering the same thing,

ma'am," Sergeant Francis said. "It's partly why he sent for Mr. Fargo, here."

The warriors were gone, the dust fading. They rode on, Fargo doing some wondering of his own.

Fort Craig had been in existence for seven years. The soldiers assigned to it were supposed to contain Apache depredations, but, although the commanding officer and those under him did their best, there was no controlling the uncontrollable.

Despite a string of forts, despite hundreds of troops, the Apaches did as they pleased.

Major Thomas Marshall was a seasoned veteran. He had dealt with Indians before. But his dealings had been with northern tribes. The Blackfeet, the Sioux, and the Bannocks were warrior cultures, the same as the Apaches, but they did not wage war every single second of every single day. They had not adopted the Apache philosophy of regarding everyone who was not an Apache, whether red or white, as an enemy.

"These infernal Mimbres are the worst of the lot," Major Marshall complained. He had invited Fargo and Patricia Haxton to his quarters for supper. Tricia had indulged in a bath and changed into a new dress she purchased at the sutler's.

Fargo had been content to strip to the waist and wash up. He had gone easy on the soap. Its scent could carry quite a ways, and Apaches had a keen sense of smell. "Some would say the Mescaleros and Chiricahuas cause as much trouble as the Mimbres," he observed.

"So some of my peers claim," Major Marshall said, "but they haven't had to deal with the Mimbres. I have. The Mimbres are totally ruthless. It will be a miracle if New Mexico is safe for settlement a hundred years from now."

An orderly in a white jacket came in bearing a tray laden with a plate heaped high with thick, sizzling slabs of beef. There were also baked potatoes, toast, and a rarity, cut green beans.

"I would imagine you must be famished," Major Marshall said pleasantly. "Normally I eat with my men, but this is a special occasion." He smiled at Tricia.

"I'm flattered, Major, but you shouldn't put yourself out on my account. Especially since, from what Sergeant Francis tells me, you and my father are not on the best of terms."

"That's putting it mildly." Marshall ran a finger across his neatly trimmed mustache. "Your father is an extremely exasperating individual."

Tricia chuckled. "I hear that a lot. He is accustomed to getting his own way. That tends to put people off."

"Frank Haxton," Major Marshall said, saying the name as someone might say "bubonic plague," "is the most opinionated, arrogant, thick-headed so-and-so I have ever met." He grinned to lessen the insult. "No offense, ma'am."

"None taken," Tricia said sincerely. "My father and I have butted heads many a time. More so in recent years, since I've taken to doing as I please. It's my right now that I'm a grown woman."

Fargo had been silent long enough. "Major, we can talk about her father later. I've come a long way at your request. I'd like to know why you sent for me."

"I'm sorry," Marshall said. "It has been remiss of me not to explain sooner. Yes, I did send specifically for you. From what I understand, you have been through this area several times and know it quite well."

"So do five or six other scouts I could name," Fargo said. "Why *me*? What is it you want me to do?"

"I would like you to persuade Frank Haxton to go back to Ohio where he belongs."

Fargo's amazement must have shown.

"Hear me out," Major Marshall urged. "This man, Haxton, has sixteen families under his spell. They have settled in a valley in the Mimbres Mountains. Paradise Valley, they call it, and they have staked out farms and are tilling the soil—"

"Tell me something I don't know," Fargo cut him off.

"Tell me why in hell you think Frank Haxton would listen to me." It was beginning to sound like the army had made a serious mistake at his expense.

"Please let me finish. You see, ordinarily I wouldn't care if a man like Haxton wanted to commit suicide. But there are women and children involved, and I owe it to them to save them, whether they want to be saved or not. They can't seem to get it through their heads that the Mimbres will exterminate them."

"Again, Major, why *me*?"

"You are familiar with Ojo Blanco, I believe?"

Fargo nodded. Ojo Blanco was almost as famous as Mangas Colorado. Extensive raids both north and south of the border were credited to him. So were countless atrocities, such as burning a Mexican school with the teacher and her young charges inside. Or the time he ambushed a wagon train and roasted the men over a fire. The women and children he drove into the desert and left with no water or food.

"He's the worst of the Mimbres, in my estimation. Word has reached me through one of my half-breed scouts that Ojo Blanco personally intends to wipe the farmers out."

Tricia interjected, "His name sounds Spanish to me."

"It is," Major Marshall confirmed. "Apaches generally have two names. Their Apache name, which they never tell outsiders, and a Spanish name. Ojo Blanco means White-Eye. It has to do with the fact his eyes are bigger than the eyes of most other Apaches, and show more of the whites." Marshall faced Fargo. "I read about your previous encounter with him in one of the files."

Fargo flashed back in memory to that fateful week, years ago, when he and a patrol he was guiding had clashed with Ojo Blanco's band, losing five troopers and killing three Apaches. "They shot at us from ambush. I never actually saw him."

"But you have a better understanding of what you are up against than most others would." Major Marshall smiled. "The main reason I sent for you, though, has nothing to do with your knowledge of the region or your knowledge of Ojo Blanco. It has to do with Danette Peters."

"Who?" Fargo had never heard of her.

"Calvin Peters is one of the farmers. Danette is his wife." Major Marshall looked at him expectantly.

"What does she have to do with anything?"

"Perhaps I have been misled, but it is my understanding you know her. From back before she married Peters. Her maiden name was Landry."

More memories welled up. Of a Conestoga filled with women, adrift on the vast prairie. Brides by mail, who had advertised in *The Heart and Hand*, a popular magazine published by a matrimonial bureau. Danette and her friends would have died if Fargo had not come along.

"Do you remember her?" Major Marshall asked, and beamed when Fargo nodded. "Excellent! She was telling the truth, then, when she said she is a friend of yours."

Fargo would not go that far. They had shared a few intimate moments, nothing more.

"It was Danette—Mrs. Peters—who suggested I send for you," Marshall said. "She has a very high opinion of your abilities."

It still made no sense to Fargo. So what if he had known one of the farmers' wives. "Tell me more about the valley and the families involved."

"There isn't much more. Haxton has them convinced they will prosper. Other than Danette Peters, they are completely under his thumb. To hear them talk, you would think Frank Haxton walks on water."

"Haven't you told him about Ojo Blanco?"

"Of course. But Haxton has an ally he can call on. One who is more powerful than all the Mimbres put together."

"Who?" Fargo asked.

"God."

Fargo waited for the officer to crack a grin or chuckle or make a humorous comment, but Marshall wasn't joking. "Don't tell me."

"Yes, he is one of *those*," the major confirmed, with a pointed glance at Tricia. "He can do no wrong because the Lord guides his every step, his every decision. Since the Lord is always right, Frank Haxton is always right. Since the Lord despises heathens, Frank Haxton despises heathens."

"Despises heathens?" Fargo could not help interrupting.

"My father has always turned a hard heart to the ungodly," Tricia said. "He says they deserve to burn in pits of hellfire."

Major Marshall leaned toward Fargo. "Are you beginning to grasp what I am up against? Haxton and his followers are convinced they are doing the Lord's will. Nothing I say will convince them otherwise." He frowned. "Don't get me wrong. I have nothing against religion, or those who are religious. But it's going to get Haxton and his people killed."

"Send in a company of your men and force them out," Fargo proposed.

"And have politicians in Washington breathing down my neck? I'd rather step barefoot into a nest of rattlesnakes."

"They have to leave. It's for their own good."

"You know that, and I know that, and so does most everyone else in the territory," Marshall said. "But there is no talking to an adobe brick, and Frank Haxton has solid adobe between his ears." Again he added, for Tricia's benefit, "No offense, ma'am."

"It's worse than I thought," she said.

"The Mimbres are as mad as mad can be. The Mimbres Mountains are their home range, you might say, and Paradise Valley is smack in the middle. So the Mimbres have gone on a killing spree, wiping out every white they come across as their way of paying the whites back for your father's folly."

Fargo thought of an obvious question. "Why haven't the Mimbres wiped out Haxton and the rest by now?"

"They tried. Ojo Blanco led the raid himself. But plows weren't the only tools the farmers brought. They have a rifle for every man, woman, and child old enough to hold one. Henry repeating rifles."

"I own one," Fargo said.

"Then you know what they are capable of. Fifteen shots a minute in the hands of someone who can shoot. Haxton's people aren't experts, but there are enough of them that they drove Ojo Blanco off. The Apaches have mostly single-shot rifles, which are no match for repeaters."

Fargo still found it hard to accept that a bunch of farmers, no matter how well armed, forced an Apache war party to tuck tail. Maybe Ojo Blanco had been overconfident and not taken enough warriors. Or maybe there was some other factor involved.

"Frank Haxton has been crowing to everyone who will listen that it was the Lord's will his people bested the Apaches, and that God will go on protecting them if the Apaches attack Paradise Valley a second time."

"That sounds like something my father would say," Tricia remarked.

"I'm sorry to ask you to put your head in a bear trap," Major Marshall said to Fargo, "but you're my last hope of ending this farce."

Fargo did not see how. Frank Haxton was no more likely to heed his advice than he had been to heed the major's. He said so.

"Ah. But you have a friend in the enemy camp, as it were. Danette Peters spoke of you in the most glowing terms. She is convinced there is no problem you can't overcome."

Tricia paused in the act of forking green beans into her mouth. "How well did you know her, if you don't mind my curiosity?"

"I saved her life once," Fargo said, and let it go at that.

"The important thing is that she trusts and respects you," Major Marshall said. "She will side with you against Haxton."

"Even so," Fargo said, "what good will it do? He'll laugh in our faces and stay right where he is. Nothing will change."

"A slim hope is better than none," Fort Craig's commanding officer declared. "I realize I'm clutching at straws, but I'm desperate. I don't want a massacre on my hands, which is exactly what I will have when Ojo Blanco strikes again."

Tricia began buttering a slice of toast. "My father beat this Ojo Blanco once. What's to stop him from doing it again?"

"Apaches never make the same mistake twice," Major Marshall answered. "Ojo Blanco didn't know about the Henrys. Now he does. He will have a surprise up his sleeve when he attacks Paradise Valley the next time. He is nothing if not devious. The outcome will be drastically different."

"I suppose you want me to head into the mountains tomorrow and have a talk with Danette," Fargo figured.

"The sooner the better, yes. But you must exercise great care. Frank Haxton does not suffer strangers."

"Not even one who is bringing his pride and joy to him?" Fargo indicated Patricia. "He'll welcome me with open arms."

"You're forgetting," Tricia said, "that he and I are not on the best of terms. He might order us out of the valley within five minutes of our arrival." She smiled oddly. "But Mrs. Peters is not the only one who owes her life to you. I will do what I can to help."

Major Marshall cheerfully rubbed his hands together. "This has worked out better than I dared hope!"

"If you ask me," Fargo said, "you're putting the cart before the horse. But I'll do what I can."

"That's all I ask." The officer pursed his lips. "There is one other thing, though. I'm afraid you'll be entirely on your own. I can't send troops along. Haxton has threatened to shoot any soldier who sets foot in his precious valley."

The door opened, framing the orderly. "Begging your pardon, sir," he said with a bow. "Sergeant Francis is here. You gave orders for him to stop by before he left for Fort Marcy."

"Show him in, Corporal."

Francis wore a clean uniform and had polished his

boots. His hat under his arm, he briskly snapped to attention. "You wanted to see me, sir?"

"Only to stress what does not need stressing," Major Marshall said. "The dispatch must get through to Colonel Arnold. I need his assistance. My command is stretched too thin, thanks to the situation at Paradise Valley. Make sure you impress that on him, no matter what."

"I will, sir. You can count on me," Sergeant Francis stated with supreme confidence. He saluted, did an about-face, and hurried out.

Major Marshall turned back to Fargo. "The rest is up to you. If you fail, New Mexico Territory will run red with blood."

5

It was hard to believe that somewhere in the Mimbres Mountains existed a valley so lush, so fertile, men were willing to die over it. The range was as stark and dry as the broad desert basin it bordered, the dreaded *Jornada del Muerto*, or the Journey of the Dead.

A newspaper editor once called New Mexico Territory the Garden of Death. Between the depredations of the Apaches and the inhospitable terrain, death was always a breath away.

Fargo agreed to a point. Yes, there were dangers, plenty of them, but there were water and abundant wildlife if one knew where to look, and beauty in the deserts and mountains if one sought it.

Now, as they wound steadily among the high peaks and crags, with the morning sun burning their backs, Fargo twisted in the saddle and gazed east across the desert. No one was on their back trail. So far the Mimbres were unaware they were there, and he would like to keep it that way.

"I would never live here in a million years," Patricia Haxton picked that moment to remark.

"How did your father hear about Paradise Valley?" Fargo asked. "Had he been here before?"

"He heard about it from a man who was going around giving talks on life in the military. A colonel somebody-or-other who spent twenty years in the army, five of them in New Mexico. The colonel was with a speaker's bureau. Do you know what they are?"

Fargo nodded. Speaker's bureaus had long lists of individuals who hired out to talk at ladies' socials, town halls, churches and the like, for a set fee. The lists included military men, explorers, writers, poets, musicians, the famous and not so famous.

"Anyway, the colonel had been to the Mimbres Mountains. He had seen the valley. It left such an impression he praised its virtues in his talk, and mentioned how he would have liked to live out the rest of his days in New Mexico if not for the Apaches," Tricia related. "My father sat up and took notice. He wouldn't stop talking about the valley. It stuck in his mind like a thorn. Next thing my mother and me knew, he announced that he was packing up and moving to New Mexico. Before long he convinced others to join him." She gazed ruefully around. "And here we are."

Harebrained notions, Fargo had observed, were as common as measles. Her father's was no different from those of the countless hordes who flocked to goldfields with the dream of striking it rich.

"I hope I don't live to regret this," Tricia said.

"You didn't need to tag along," Fargo replied. "I could have left you at the fort. Major Marshall would see that you got safely to Albuquerque. From there you could take a stage anywhere you wanted go."

"I've come this far," Tricia said, "I might as well see it through. Besides, for all my father's faults, I miss him and my mother. They were right about that worthless lunkhead I married. I should have listened."

The land shimmered in a heat haze that distorted objects in the distance. A few lizards skittered from their path, and a pair of hawks in search of prey soared on outstretched wings.

At noon they stopped for a short rest. Fargo took the water skin from his saddle and offered it to Tricia, saying, "Only a few mouthfuls."

She carefully raised it to her lips and rolled the water in her mouth, then swallowed. "Funny how we take things for granted. Back in Ohio we had a well and there was a river nearby. Water everywhere."

"Will you go back after you have seen your folks?"

"I don't know. I've heard good things about California. They say parts of it are sunny all year, and the people are easy to get along with. Or there is always Oregon Country."

Fargo carried the water skin to the Ovaro and went to hang it from the saddle horn. A bright gleam high in the mountains caught his eye. It was there and it was gone, a flash of sunlight off metal, unless he was mistaken. He tried to spot the source but couldn't. It worried him. Some Apaches had spyglasses. The Mimbres were bound to be watching the approaches to the valley, ready to ambush any whites who came along.

"Mount up," Fargo directed, and rode north for a mile, opposite the direction they should go.

If Tricia noticed, she did not say anything. Eventually Fargo turned west, and later, southwest. Several times an hour he stopped to check their back trail.

Evening found them well into the Mimbres. Fargo had a particular spot in mind to stop for the night, a spring nestled at the base of a high canyon wall. He stripped the horses, gathered fuel for their fire, and put a pot of coffee on to boil.

Tricia was brushing her hair. "You're right handy," she said with a smirk. "Do you do laundry too?"

"I'll leave that to you." Fargo began cutting some of his pemmican into pieces for the soup he would make. He would do no hunting until they reached the valley. The sound of a shot carried a long distance.

"May I ask you something?"

"So long as it's not personal." Fargo plopped one of the pieces into his mouth and rolled it with his tongue. He tasted the chokecherries that had been mixed with the buffalo meat and fat.

"What are the odds of us making it out alive?"

"*Now* you ask," Fargo marveled.

"I cross bridges when I come to them," Tricia said. "Be honest with me. I really want to know."

Fargo gave it to her plain. "Fifty-fifty, or less."

"Yet here you are, risking your life for people you don't even know."

"It's my job. Don't make more out of it than there is." Fargo had enough pemmican ready. He dropped the pieces in a pan he had already filled with water.

"What will you do if my father won't listen to reason?"

"Like you, I cross bridges when I come to them," Fargo hedged. He had talked to Major Marshall privately before they left, and the major had asked the same thing.

"I bring it up," Marshall had said, "to stress a point. You have more leeway than I do. You work for the army but you are not *in* the army and can't be held to account for things the politicians in Washington might not like."

"Yet another reason you sent for me," Fargo had deduced.

"You have a reputation for getting things done no matter what it takes. This is one of those jobs where it might take a lot."

"Spell it out," Fargo had said.

"Do whatever you have to."

"Anything?"

"You will not be prosecuted. You have my personal guarantee. General Hathaway is aware of the situation, and he has the ear of the President."

"It goes that high up?"

"It pays to keep an eye on situations like this. You never know. The newspapers might get hold of the story, and some of them love to paint the government and the army as the root of all evil."

"I won't kill any of them if I can help it," Fargo had promised.

"Just remember. Apaches make convenient scapegoats." The major had lowered his voice. "I'm truly sorry to place the burden on your shoulders, but there is no one else I can turn to. If it were up to me, I would take my men in and bring Haxton and his followers out at gunpoint. But my hands are officially tied."

"I understand," Fargo had said.

"For what it's worth," Major Marshall said solemnly,

"I am in your debt. If there is ever anything I can do for you, anything at all, you have but to ask."

On that vow they parted.

Fargo had debated whether to tell Tricia and decided not to. Better, he felt, if he kept it to himself. He stirred the soup, then looked up to find her studying him. In the rosy glow of the fire she looked inviting, sitting there with her hands behind her, her hair cascading past her shoulders, her breasts jutting against her dress. A constriction formed in his throat. He coughed to clear it and said, "Something else on your mind?"

"I was thinking of the other night," Tricia said softly, "and the two of us. Remember?"

"It's not something a man forgets." Fargo checked the coffee. The water was bubbling, but it would be a while yet.

"We won't be able to once we reach Paradise Valley," Tricia mentioned. "I'll be staying with my parents."

"That's good to know," Fargo said. Out of the corner of his eye he saw her frown, and he smiled inwardly.

"That was a hint."

"Don't worry. I won't touch you once we get there," Fargo assured her. "I wouldn't want you to get into trouble with your folks."

"How considerate," Tricia said archly. "But that wasn't quite what I meant."

Fargo acted as if he had not heard her and went on cooking. The crackle of the fire and the hiss of the coffeepot lent the night an aura of friendliness. The high canyon walls sheltered them from the wind, and from hostile prying eyes. A crescent of vegetation bordering the spring served as added protection.

Tricia shared tidbits about her life growing up on a farm. How she had learned to milk the cows when she was but seven years old, learned to ride when she was eight, learned to sew and embroider by twelve. "All the things my parents taught me, all the time I spent learning the upkeep of hearth and home, and I couldn't keep my husband from straying."

Fargo wished he had some whiskey. "It's pointless to flog a dead horse. What's done is done."

"Easy for you to say." Tricia swiveled on the small boulder she was perched on and stretched her long, willowy legs. "I don't care to become a spinster."

"You'll be married before you're twenty-five," Fargo predicted. To nip her maudlin reminiscence in the bud, he rose, came around the fire, and tucked at the knees behind her. She was gazing at the stars, lost in her guilt.

"Has there ever been something you wanted so much you could not bear to live without it?"

"Yes." Fargo slid his hands to her breasts and cupped them, eliciting a startled gasp. He nuzzled her neck and nipped her earlobe, and she giggled girlishly.

"Here I thought you didn't want me."

"Has anyone ever mentioned you talk too much?" Fargo pulled her to him and molded his mouth to hers in a kiss that lingered on and on, while they explored one another with their hands.

Tricia did not resist when he raised her to her feet and pressed against her back. "What about supper?" she teased.

"It can wait."

Fargo hiked the hem of her dress and her petticoat, and loosened her cotton drawers but did not take them off.

"You want to take me like this?"

"Why not?"

"You make a girl feel positively naughty." Tricia grinned. "I'm not complaining, mind you. Quite the contrary."

"That's nice," Fargo said, and was in her in one swift, fluid stroke. She had not felt him undo his belt and his pants, and it caught her by surprise. She bent her spine into a bow, and groaned.

"Mmmmmmmm. Dessert before the meal, is that what this is?"

Holding her hips, Fargo commenced stroking in and out. He took her hard and fast and she responded in kind, bending her head for him to kiss her and cupping her own breasts and pinching her nipples. Their passion was as hot as the fire, and intense with mutual need.

"Yesssssss," Tricia cooed. "Don't stop! I'm almost there! Just a little more!" She mewed like a kitten, then suddenly cried out and bucked wildly, thrusting herself at him as if seeking to knock his legs out from under him.

Fargo felt her spurt, felt her contractions, felt his thighs grow damp. He pounded into her until his release would not be denied. She shuddered and reached back to sink her fingernails in his legs. Afterward, they stood shaking and spent, Tricia leaning on him for support.

"That was nice. Do you suppose we could do it again once or twice before morning?"

"I might if you twist my arm."

Tricia tittered. "I know a better way to persuade you." Grinning, she seductively slid her hand between his legs. "What's this? Don't worry. I won't twist it. We wouldn't want to damage you."

Dawn came much too soon. As was his habit, Fargo awoke before sunrise and lay snuggled against Tricia, listening to a rock wren sing. They had spent most of the night making love.

A chickadee and its mate alighted at the water's edge, quickly drank, and flew off into the brush.

Fargo detached himself from Tricia's warm body. Everything appeared normal enough, but in Apache country normal was often misleading. He rose and scoured the canyon. Lower down a doe and her fawn were grazing. The deer were no doubt thirsty, but would not come near the spring until they were gone. He saw the tracks of a curious kangaroo rat that had ventured near them while they slept.

The Ovaro nickered and stamped. It was thirsty, too. Fargo pulled out the picket pins and brought the horses to the spring. Kneeling, he took off his hat, cupped his hands, and splashed cool, invigorating water on his face and hair. He had put his hat back on and was rising when he saw the footprints. Three of them, moccasin tracks, partial prints showing mostly the heels and the balls of the feet, and the imprint of a knee, showing where, days ago, an Apache had done exactly as Fargo just had.

Rising, Fargo went to Tricia and gently shook her shoulder. He could not say why, but he had a sudden, urgent need to get out of there. He blamed it on nerves caused by the footprints, but it went deeper than that. It was a feeling, an intuition, a sense that their sanctuary was no sanctuary at all, and if one Mimbre knew about the spring, every Mimbre did. Sooner or later one or more would happen by.

Tricia smacked her red lips and rolled onto her side. "Let me be. I need more sleep."

"Tell that to the Apaches."

Her eyes snapped open and she was instantly, fully awake. Sitting up, she gazed anxiously about, then said irritably, "I don't see any. It wasn't nice to scare me like that."

"I'll saddle the horses. Be ready to go in five minutes."

"What about our morning coffee?" Tricia groused. "I can't function without it." She fussed with her hair. "I must look a sight. At least permit me to wash out before we go."

"Five minutes," Fargo repeated, and picked up his saddle blanket and saddle. The wren had stopped warbling, and the doe and her fawn had disappeared. He hurriedly prepared to ride out, and had both mounts ready when Tricia walked sleepily over, stifling a yawn.

"How can you have so much vigor and vim after last night? You about wore me out."

"I like being alive," Fargo said.

The Ovaro and her horse were both staring down the canyon. Somewhere in the vicinity of the canyon mouth a jay squawked. Sparrows took swift wing.

Without delay Fargo kicked dirt over the charred embers from last night's fire. He shoved the bay's reins at Tricia, and with the Ovaro's reins in his left hand, headed up the canyon, not down it, at a brisk walk.

"Where the blazes are you going?" Tricia wanted to know. "We came in down below, remember?"

"We have company."

Tricia did not waste another moment. She hastened after him, saying, "Why didn't you say so sooner? Apaches, you think? Or someone else?"

"We'll find out soon enough." Fargo had no idea what they would find at the upper end of the canyon. Hopefully, a way out. He climbed twenty yards, stopped, and swore. A hundred yards higher the canyon ended at the bottom of a bluff so sheer that scaling it would be impossible. Much closer grew a solitary willow hemmed by brush. He led the Ovaro to a gap between the willow and the canyon wall.

No sooner did Tricia come to a stop next to him than Fargo thrust the Ovaro's reins at her. "Hold these."

"Why? Where are you off to?"

Fargo's action spoke for him. Leaning the Henry against the trunk, he stepped under a low branch, reached as high he could, and jumped. Catching hold, he swung his legs up, balanced himself, and climbed from branch to branch. He did not have high to climb.

Fully twenty Mimbres were riding up the canyon in single file. Most had rifles. Neither their postures nor their attitudes betrayed any suspicion that they knew Fargo and Tricia were there. They were relaxed and at ease. Why should they not be, so deep in Mimbre territory? Other than the settlers in Paradise Valley, few whites were brave enough, or stupid enough, to penetrate this deep into their heartland.

Fargo pressed flush with the trunk so they would be less likely to spot him. The lead rider interested him.

The man's eyes were as large as walnuts, with a lot of white showing, the trait that distinguished Ojo Blanco. Short and stocky, the widely feared Mimbre leader wore a brown long-sleeved shirt, a breechclout, and knee-high moccasins. A wide band circled his shoulder-length black hair. His features were typical of Apaches in general; swarthy and rugged, although, in keeping with his large eyes, he also had big ears and a prominent hooked nose that lent him the aspect of a predatory bird. He rode up to the spring and lithely dismounted.

Fargo held his breath. If any of the warriors glanced down, they were bound to notice the fresh sign. But more and more came up and swung to the ground without paying it any particular attention. Soon the space around the spring was filled with Apaches and their animals, hopefully obliterating all the tracks Tricia and he had left.

The Mimbres took turns drinking, seven or eight at a time. They would squat and dip their hands and take a few sips, and that was all. They did not drink their fill, as parched whites and Mexicans would do. Dividing into small groups, they hunkered in circles to talk and joke.

Seeing them like that, Fargo was reminded that Apaches were not the fiends incarnate most whites made them out to be. Apaches were human beings, with human flaws and weaknesses. Nothing more, nothing less.

Ojo Blanco stepped onto a boulder and launched into what amounted to being, for an Apache, a long speech. He talked for over a minute, with much gesturing, and kept pointing south—toward Paradise Valley, Fargo guessed. Whatever Ojo Blanco said brought grunts and murmurs of approval from the rest.

They were planning their next raid, Fargo guessed. But would it be sooner, or later? A lot of lives depended on the Apaches holding off a while.

A rustling sound drew Fargo's gaze to the base of the willow. Tricia was staring up expectantly. The horses were where he had left them, their reins dangling.

"What are you doing up there?" she whispered. "What do you see?"

"I told you to stay with the horses," Fargo whispered down.

"You most certainly did not. All you did was hand me your reins. I want to climb up with you."

Fargo spiked with annoyance. "Go keep an eye on them. We don't want them wandering off."

"If you insist," Tricia said sulkily, "but you don't have to bite my head off." She did not move. "You still haven't told me what you see."

57

"An Apache war party."

Tricia blanched and put a hand to her throat. "How many? What do we do? If they spot us, we're goners."

"If we lie low, they won't," was Fargo's hope. He glanced toward the spring and his gut balled into a knot. One of the Apaches was bent low at the water's edge, at the very spot where he had knelt to drink.

The Mimbre was about to dip his hands in the water when he froze. He ran his fingers over the ground and said something that brought two others to his side.

Fargo's skin prickled. Their lives were precariously poised on the cusp of discovery. All it would take was for the warriors to fan out across the canyon floor and advance up it to the willow. He could retreat to the bluff, but he would only delay the inevitable.

Tricia was still below. "What's the matter? Why do you look like someone just stepped on your grave?"

The warrior who was bent low hollered to Ojo Blanco. Fargo caught the words *pindah lickoyee*, which in the Apache tongue meant white-eyes, or white men. Ojo Blanco went over. Other warriors watched with interest.

"Skye?" Tricia whispered.

"Do as I told you, damn it," Fargo snapped, not taking his eyes off the war party. Ojo Blanco had straightened and was scratching his chin.

"Must you use that tone with me?" Tricia indignantly asked, but she wheeled and did as he had instructed.

Fargo froze. Ojo Blanco was staring up the canyon. Had the Apache leader spotted him? No, for a moment later Ojo Blanco gestured at four warriors, and the four cat-footed past the spring and started to spread out, examining the ground as they went. The four best trackers, Fargo figured. Warriors every bit as skilled as he was. The outcome was inevitable.

Suddenly one stopped and sank onto a knee, and yipped like a coyote. Immediately, the entire war party gathered excitedly about him. They were like a pack of wolves that had caught the scent of newly spilled blood.

Fargo wanted to beat his head against the tree for not getting out of there sooner. The five minutes had been four minutes too many. Now they were in for it. The tracks their horses had made were as plain as plain could be.

The Apaches had them trapped.

6

Ojo Blanco swung his arm and shouted, and the Mimbres started to fan out across the canyon, just as Faro expected. Quickly, he lowered himself from limb to limb, grabbed hold of the lowest branch, and swung lightly to the ground.

Tricia had gathered up both reins and was turning as he ran up to the Ovaro. "What in the world? What's wrong?"

Fargo did not answer. He did not have a moment to lose. He opened his saddlebags and found the fire steel and flint he used to start fires. Then he raced a dozen feet down the canyon and frantically tore at the brush to gather a pile of kindling. In seconds he had plenty. Kneeling, he held the steel and the flint close to the pile and struck them together. Sparks jumped, and a few tiny wisps of smoke appeared. He struck again and again, puffing lightly when one of the sparks ignited. One of the bright orange spots grew into a flame. The flame multiplied and became two, then three. Tearing grass out, he added it bit by bit until the pile caught. The flames spread rapidly, like a swarm of colorful spiders.

The vegetation was bone-dry, brown from lack of moisture. It was a fire waiting to happen. Fargo stepped back as the breeze fanned the flames to the right and left. He had created a skirmish line of his own, a skirmish line of living flame. The speed with which it spread was astonishing.

Whirling, Fargo sprinted to the horses.

Tricia was aghast, her eyes wide with fright. "What have you done? Have you gone mad? We'll be burned alive!"

"Mount up and be ready to ride when I tell you." Fargo shoved the steel and flint in his saddlebag. He took the Ovaro's reins and forked leather. "What are you waiting for?" he demanded.

"But the fire—" She motioned in confusion.

"The wind is blowing down the canyon, not up it," Fargo enlightened her. "It will drive the fire toward the Apaches, not toward us." And when it reached the mouth of the canyon, where the belt of vegetation ended, it would die for lack of fuel.

"You're trying to burn them alive?" Tricia made it sound like the foulest deed ever conceived.

"Do you honestly think they'll stand there and let that happen?" The notion was too ridiculous. No, the Apaches would do what any sensible person would do; they would fly to their horses and retreat down the canyon ahead of the flames and the smoke.

The smoke. It was the key. Either it would save them, or they would die. Already thick plumes rose into the sky. Plumes that billowed and linked and would soon became a choking, acrid cloud extending from one canyon wall to the other.

Tricia was on the bay, anxiety written large on her countenance. "I get it now! The smoke will hide us so we can get away."

"Stay by my side," Fargo cautioned. "If we're separated—" He did not finish the statement.

Her throat bobbed, and she paled. "No need to say more. I will stick to you like tar. I promise."

Fargo stared at the spreading smoke. It would not be long. Less than a minute, if that.

"I'm sorry I have given you such a hard time," Tricia said. "But the way you were acting had me scared."

"Get ready." Fargo firmed his grip on his reins and bent forward over the saddle horn.

"Please don't hold it against me," Tricia prattled on. Fear had turned her mouth into a babbling brook.

61

The smoke was almost thick enough.

"What will they do to me if they catch me?" Tricia licked her lips, and said softly, "I shudder to think."

"Now!" Fargo cried. Leaning to the side, he gave the bay a sharp smack that sent it bolting toward the smoke before it realized what it was doing. He used his spurs and within heartbeats was alongside it. The two horses galloped hell-bent for leather down the canyon.

Fargo was worried the horses might balk, especially the bay, but both plunged into the smoke without hesitation. Side by side they sped for their lives, the drum of heavy hooves echoing off the high walls. Crackling flames were everywhere. To avoid them, they had to constantly rein to either side.

Shouts punctured the smoke. Horses whinnied. Vague shapes were briefly outlined and then were gone.

From the sound of things, Fargo reckoned the fire had confused and scattered the Apaches, exactly as he planned. They were running for their mounts, some of which had run off, stranding some of the warriors afoot.

Suddenly a Mimbre materialized in front of the Ovaro. The warrior was groping through the smoke cloud, which was now as thick as fog. Hearing the Ovaro and the bay, the Mimbre turned. Apparently he believed they were fellow Mimbres because he did not resort to his rifle. The next instant the truth hit him and he jerked his rifle up to shoot.

Fargo rode the man down. The Ovaro slammed into him like a four-legged battering ram and the Apache was hurled head over moccasins into the billowing gray by the brutal force of the impact. Fargo kept going. Tricia was still at his side, a determined set to her face, her eyes narrowed against the stinging cloud.

Close to their right, an Apache yelled. Another answered from off to the left. A riderless horse appeared, but veered away from them and was lost to view.

Fargo had no idea how far they had gone. He estimated they were past the spring, about midway down the canyon. He had hoped the smoke would thin, but no such luck. Boulders loomed, and he reined sharply to avoid them. For a few seconds he lost sight of Tricia. Reining back again, he looked for her but she did not reappear. He slowed and yelled her name but there was no answer. He slowed even more and yelled again.

Damn. Fargo rose in the stirrups and peered hard into the smoke, but all he saw was more smoke. "Tricia! Where are you?" He was taking a risk the Apaches would pinpoint him by his voice, but he had to find her quickly or any chance they had of escaping would be dashed.

Suddenly, there was a break in the cloud, a small patch of clear air, and at its center a mounted warrior with his rifle rising. The Mimbre's large eyes lit with fierce exultation as he went to take aim.

It was Ojo Blanco.

Hauling on the reins, Fargo narrowly missed colliding with the Mimbre leader's horse. They were so close their legs brushed. So close, Fargo grabbed the barrel of Ojo Blanco's rifle and wrenched it from the Apache's grasp as he went by. The rifle went off, but the slug went wide.

Then Fargo was past and applying his spurs. Quick as thought, Ojo Blanco wheeled his mount and gave chase. The Apache's mount was incredibly swift. In a twinkling, it overtook the Ovaro.

Ojo Blanco's hand flashed to a knife at his hip. Whipping it out, he slashed at Fargo.

Fargo twisted aside. He still had hold of the barrel of the Mimbre's rifle, and he swung it like a club. The stock caught Ojo Blanco full in the face. Instinctively, he reached up to ward off any other blows. Fargo swung the rifle again, hitting him across the chest. With a howl like an enraged bear, Ojo Blanco tumbled.

Fargo threw the rifle down. Twisting in the saddle, he saw neither Ojo Blanco nor Tricia. Part of him wanted to stop and search for her, but that would result in certain capture. On he galloped, telling himself that he was doing the right thing. He would be of no use to her if he was staked out over an anthill with his skin stripped from his body.

Apaches still shouted, and their horses still whinnied but the sounds were all behind him.

Abruptly, the smoke thinned. The flames were fewer. Fargo burst out of the cloud, his chest aching, his eyes smarting. He came to the mouth and drew rein to gaze back up the canyon. As yet none of the war party was in sight, and still no sign of Tricia. He cupped a hand to his mouth to call her name, then thought better of advertising where he was.

Angry that he had lost her, Fargo swore. Either she had become disoriented in the smoke, or the Mimbres had her, or her horse had gone down. All he could do was wait, but not there.

To his right a slope canted toward the top of the canyon wall. Fargo went up it at a trot, earth and stones cascading from under the Ovaro's hooves. He came on a game trail used by deer and other animals. It made things easier. Shortly, he was at the canyon rim, and staring down into a slate soup.

The breeze had slackened and the smoke hung heavy in the air. Here and there flames showed against the gray.

Several riderless horses came to the canyon's mouth and fled down the mountain. Then six mounted Mimbres appeared. Two went after the riderless animals while the rest waited. Soon they were joined by others, some on horseback and some on foot.

Gigging the Ovaro away from the rim so the Apaches would not spot it, Fargo slid down. He removed his hat, flattened, and crawled to the edge. He counted sixteen Mimbres. Some had smoke in their lungs and were coughing and wheezing. Another appeared. Behind him trailed two more.

That left one Mimbre unaccounted for.

Ojo Blanco was the last to emerge, and he was not alone. He was on the bay, behind Tricia, an arm locked around her waist. At sight of him some of the other Apaches whooped. Then they gathered in close to inspect his captive.

Patricia Haxton seemed to be in shock. Blood trickled from a corner of her mouth, and the sleeve of her dress was torn. Ojo Blanco seized her by the hair and said something that made the rest of the Mimbres smirk.

Fargo could easily pick Ojo Blanco off, but what good would it do him? The bay was hemmed by warriors. Tricia could not flee. Wiser to trail them and wait for a chance to free her later. Provided she lived that long.

Ojo Blanco had drawn his knife. He yanked Tricia's head up and placed the tip to her throat.

Fargo had left his Henry in the saddle scabbard. Coiling his legs under him so he could retrieve it, he paused when he saw Ojo Blanco laugh and slice the blade across Tricia's throat. Or so it appeared from his high elevation. But the razor-sharp steel never touched her skin. Ojo Blanco only pretended to slit her jugular.

The Mimbres were greatly amused.

Then Ojo Blanco twisted Tricia's head around so they were face-to-face and spoke to her, and to Fargo's mild surprise, she stirred and answered. Evidently Ojo Blanco knew English. Some Apaches did. Some, like the famed Mangas Colorado, spoke three or more languages; their own tongue, Spanish, English, and a tongue or two from other tribes. The notion that they were stupid savages, widespread among whites, could not be more wrong.

Ojo Blanco replaced his knife. He shook Tricia and snarled something at her. Whatever her answer was, it displeased him, and he angrily cuffed her across the cheek. He pointed at the smoke and said more, and she shook her head. Furious, Ojo Blanco smacked her three times in swift succession and she slumped, half conscious.

What was that about? Fargo wondered. And it hit him. Ojo Blanco was asking about *him*. The tracks had told the Mimbres she was not alone, and they wanted to get their hands on the man she was with.

The warriors on horseback climbed down and a general council was held. Unlike some tribes where a leader's word was always obeyed, Apache warriors were free to do whatever they pleased whenever they pleased. They were under no obligation to do as their leaders wanted. The will of their leaders often prevailed, but only after they convinced their fellow warriors that their way was the best way. An Apache could fight or not fight, could go on the warpath or not go on the warpath, could refuse to do anything he did not want to do.

Apaches cherished their freedom above all else, a trait, ironically, they shared with the whites out to exterminate them.

The council ended. The fire was dying and the smoke had thinned to where sections of the canyon were visible, stretches of blistered and charred vegetation. Hardly a blade of grass had been spared.

As they had done at the spring, the Mimbres now spread out across the canyon floor until a skirmish line ran from wall to wall, with ten feet or so between each warrior. At a shout from Ojo Blanco, they advanced up the canyon, checking behind boulders and poking in what was left of the blackened thickets.

Ojo Blanco stayed behind, observing.

The Mimbres must think the fire had taken his life, Fargo guessed, and were hunting for his body. Once they reached the bluff at the far end, they would realize the truth. That would take a while, though.

Tricia sagged against Ojo Blanco, her arms limp at her sides. He shook her head, but she did not lift her eyes.

Fargo watched the other warriors. He had a brainstorm. It was reckless. It might get him killed. But with Tricia's life in the bargain, the risk was justified. Sliding from the rim, he stood and stepped into the stirrups, and headed down the slope. He took care not to show himself until he was two-thirds of the way down.

Ojo Blanco had not moved. The other Mimbres were well up the canyon and in a couple of minutes would reach the spring.

Bending low over the saddle again, Fargo continued to descend. At the bottom he drew rein in the shadow of the rock wall. He drew his Colt but did not cock it. A shot would alert the others.

Ojo Blanco's back was to the mouth of the canyon.

Tricia was facing Fargo, but her hair hung over her eyes and she did not know he was there.

The line of Mimbres was almost out of sight. Fargo tensed, and the Ovaro, by long habit sensitive to his changes in posture, raised its head.

Ojo Blanco shook Tricia again and said something, his words distinct in the stillness. "I ask you one more time, woman. Where is the white dog you were with? Did he escape us?"

Tricia mumbled something.

"You must talk louder, bitch."

Brushing the hair from her face, Tricia looked up. In addition to the blood on her mouth she had a welt on her forehead and dark bruises on both cheeks. "Stop calling me that."

With a feral snarl, Ojo Blanco hurled her from the bay. She landed on her shoulder and cried out in pain. He laughed and pointed at her. "Learn your place, woman, or I will hurt you more. I will hurt you so that you cry and beg me to stop hurting you."

Tricia slowly rolled onto her back, favoring her sore shoulder. "You like hurting people, don't you?"

"When I must."

"You are like all your kind. Savage through and through." Tricia rose on her elbow. "No better than animals."

Ojo Blanco's features mirrored contempt. "You whites. You think Apaches are less than you because we protect our land and our people. Yet you would do as we do if we did to you as you do to us."

"We are not like your kind at all. We do not murder innocent women and children. We do not torture."

"You lie. White men have killed *Shis-Inday* women. White men have killed *Shis-Inday* children."

Apaches did not call themselves Apaches, Fargo knew. It was a name bestowed on them by another tribe. Among themselves they were the *Shis-Inday*, or Men of the Woods. Contrary to popular belief, Apaches did not dwell high amid the rocky crags of their domain, but in the dense forests on the slopes below.

"But I wasn't one of them. You have no reason to hurt me, no reason to want to kill me."

"I have the best reason," Ojo Blanco said. "You are white."

"And you are a bigot," Tricia bristled. "I expect no less from someone who was brought up to kill without being killed and steal without being caught. You see, I know about your people."

"You know nothing," Ojo Blanco said.

By now the rest of the Mimbres were out of sight. Fargo rode slowly out of the shadows, making straight for Ojo Blanco. In order that Ojo Blanco might not hear the Ovaro until the pinto was almost on top of him, Fargo moved at a slow walk.

Almost instantly, Tricia saw him. To her credit, she did not betray him by calling out or motioning. Instead, she raised her voice to mask his approach. "I know more than you think! I know you tried to wipe out my father and his friends in Paradise Valley! I know that they drove you off! I know you hate whites for hate's sake, and are no better than the whites who killed your women and children!"

Her tirade rolled off Ojo Blanco like water off a duck's back. His feathers were not the least bit ruffled. She paused to take a breath, and he asked, "Why do you shout when I am so near you?"

Fargo only had fifteen feet to go.

But Ojo Blanco was no fool; he stiffened and whipped around, and on spying Fargo, swept his rifle up. Fargo lashed his reins, but he could not close the gap in time. He must shoot and grab Tricia and ride like hell to outrace the rest of the war party.

Then Tricia sprang up and wrapped her arms about Ojo Blanco, spoiling his aim. He pushed her, but she would not let go, so he drew back his foot to kick her.

By then the Ovaro was next to the bay. Ojo Blanco perceived his peril and shifted, much too late. Fargo smashed the Colt's barrel against the stocky Mimbre's temple. Three times metal connected with flesh and bone. Ojo Blanco's rifle fell from nerveless fingers and he melted from the bay like so much hot wax.

"Get on!" Fargo commanded, holding the bay's reins so it would not run off.

Tricia did not need to be told twice. She clutched at the bay's saddle horn, missed, and clutched again. The bay shied, but she managed to cling on and swing up, her dress swirling, inadvertently treating him to a tantalizing glimpse of her long legs and exquisite thighs.

Reining the Ovaro around, Fargo urged, "Ride!", and did so, exploding out of the canyon at a gallop. Neck and neck with the bay, he flew to the south. They had to put as many miles as they could behind them before the Mimbres gave chase.

Tricia's close brush with death had taught her a lesson. She did not chatter like a chipmunk but rode in grim earnest.

Half a mile, and no pursuit. A mile fell behind them, and not a trace of dust anywhere in the distance.

Fargo slowed. Tricia followed his example. Their horses were caked with sweat and dust. So were they.

"We were lucky," Fargo remarked.

"I thought I was done for. When we were separated in all that smoke were the scariest moments of my life."

"It's over," Fargo said, hoping she would not start bawling. "We survived, and that's what matters."

"Their leader hit me." Tricia lightly touched her swollen lip. "There was nothing I could do. I was at his mercy. Why he didn't kill me, I will never know."

"Maybe he took a shine to you," Fargo said, when in all likelihood Ojo Blanco had been saving her for a darker purpose. Ojo Blanco was notorious for inflicting pain on his enemies before he killed them.

"It was the last straw," Tricia declared. "I have had my fill of New Mexico Territory. I'll spend a few days with my folks, but then I am leaving and I am never coming back. I only hope I can talk sense into them and make them go with me."

"If *I* had any sense I would take you back to Fort Craig," Fargo said. But they were over halfway to the valley, and Ojo Blanco was behind them.

"You saved me. Again. I will never forget that."

Uncomfortable being praised, Fargo said, "You did all right, grabbing him like you did."

Tricia giggled. "I did, didn't I? To tell you the truth, I did it without thinking. If I had it to do over again, I might not."

The sun was at its zenith when Fargo drew rein on a boulder-strewn ridge. He sat with his back to a tall slab to watch their trail, and passed his water skin to her. "You first."

Gratefully accepting, Tricia gulped greedily.

"Don't overdo it. It has to last."

"But we'll reach the valley the day after tomorrow," Tricia objected. "There is plenty of water there." She went to drink more, but lowered the water skin instead. "I'm doing it again, aren't I?" She held it out to him. "Sorry. Some habits are hard to break, I reckon."

"You learn from your mistakes. Many don't, and they pay with an early grave." Fargo came across their bleached bones all the time. Emigrants who ventured into the wild thinking they could take care of themselves. Misguided souls who judged the West by the East and learned at death's door that the West was far deadlier than the East could ever be.

Fargo lifted the water skin. He swallowed only enough to wet his mouth and throat. Resting his head against the boulder, he closed his eyes. He could do with a nap. Heat sapped the vitality, and the mountains were an oven.

"I feel sleepy," Tricia echoed. "It must be the sun, and all we have been through today."

A sudden sound from the south slope of the ridge snapped Fargo out of his drowsiness and brought him to his feet in a bound with his hand on the Colt. A clattering sound that might be dislodged rocks sliding down the slope.

"Don't tell me they've found us!" Tricia whispered fearfully. "Don't let them get their hands on me!"

Before Fargo could answer, a man stepped from between two boulders holding a leveled shotgun. The twin hammers were already thumbed back. He pointed his cannon at Fargo's belly.

"How do you do, mister? Nice day if it rains." The man chortled. "By the way, so much as twitch and you're dead."

7

There was a saying on the frontier: buckshot meant burying. A slug from a revolver or a rifle was not always fatal, but a blast from a shotgun loaded with buckshot could blow a man apart.

To have twin muzzles trained on him was enough to dissuade Fargo from going for his Colt. At that range he would be turned into a sieve—what was left of him.

The man holding the shotgun was dressed in homespun and boots. His clothes were well worn from long use, his boots scuffed. He had a stout build and was darkly tanned from long hours spent outdoors. His shirt, open at the collar, bristled with a mat of chest hair. Hair as black as the thatch that poked from under his short-brimmed hat. His wide face split in a smirk as he said, "My name is Calvin. We didn't count on running into anyone else in these parts. Not many whites come this far into the mountains. They're too afraid of the Apaches."

Remembering what Major Marshall had told him, Fargo put two and two together and said, "Your last name is Peters, isn't it? And you're from Paradise Valley."

Tricia had also frozen, but now she brightened and exclaimed, "Then you must know my father!"

"And who might you be, girl?"

Before Patricia could answer, several more men appeared. They were all dressed like Calvin. Unlike him, they were all armed with Henry rifles, the brass receivers gleaming brightly in the sunlight. In the lead was a tall man who held his head high and his shoulders thrown back with an air of forced dignity; he moved as if he owned the earth and everything on it. Years of hard toil, of handling a heavy plow and working tirelessly from dawn to dusk, had bronzed him as they had Calvin.

"Father!" Patricia cried in delight, and with her arms wide, ran to greet him.

Frank Haxton stopped short and blinked in astonishment, his self-assured manner briefly shattered. "Tricia?" he said uncertainly, not believing the evidence of his eyes. "How can this be?"

Embracing him, Tricia pressed a cheek to his chest and said, choked with emotion, "It's so wonderful to see you again! I am so sorry for all the sorrow I caused you and mother."

The other farmers were as surprised as their leader. Calvin lowered his shotgun but kept it pointed in Fargo's general direction.

"You are the last person I expected to find in the middle of this godforsaken wilderness," Frank Haxton said.

Fargo noticed that Haxton did not embrace her or show any of the warmth she showed. In fact, the man acted uncomfortable at the contact with his own flesh and blood.

"I had to come! You and mother were right. My husband was worthless. He ran out on me."

In a stern tone, Frank Haxton declared, "Never put your trust in the ungodly daughter. How many times did I tell you that?"

Tricia's eyes were closed, and tears trickled from under her long lashes. "I am sorry I ever doubted you. I guess I'm too willful for my own good."

Haxton's face softened and he gingerly laid a hand on her shoulder. "There, there. The young often make mistakes like yours. It comes from not putting your trust in your Maker."

"Where's mother? I can't wait to see her again, too."

The comment brought a frown to Haxton, who looked up, his dark eyes boring into Fargo. "What's this, then?

Have you picked up another stray in your travels? Or is this a new husband?"

Dabbing at her face, Tricia stepped back. "Goodness, no. He's a friend. Be nice to him. He saved my life a short while ago, and has taken his life in his hands to bring me to you."

"Is that a fact?" Frank Haxton said with an air of suspicion. "He saved your life how, exactly?"

"From an Apache called Ojo Blanco."

Haxton and the other farmers glanced at one another, and Haxton gripped her by both arms and nearly lifted her off the ground. "Ojo Blanco? The devil incarnate? You have seen him? You are sure it was him?"

"I was as close to him as I am to you," Tricia said. "He spoke to me. He told me who he was."

"And you are still alive?" Haxton raised his face to the heavens. "Thank you, Lord, for preserving my child." Then, still holding her, he addressed her as if she were ten years old. "Think carefully, child. Was there another white girl with him? Did you see anything of Lucy Harker?"

"Who? No, Father. Only other Apaches."

A man to Haxton's left bowed his head and said forlornly, "Then the heathens have killed her. God rest her soul."

"We don't know that they have, Elias," Haxton responded. "Have faith, and all will turn out well." To Tricia he said, "This is Elias Harker. Lucy is his daughter. She disappeared yesterday morning when she went to fetch water."

Fargo broke his silence. "You have been tracking the Apaches who took her?"

Haxton seemed strangely annoyed by the question. "We are farmers, sir, not woodsmen. We found no tracks. But one of my people spotted Apaches north of our valley the night before the girl vanished."

Fargo was struck by the futility of their search. They were blundering around like blind mice, with no idea where the girl was, hoping by some miracle to stumble across her. "Maybe I can help." He introduced himself.

"I've scouted for the army, and I have some experience tracking." Which shaved the truth by half. He figured Haxton would be happy to have his services but his measure of the man needed adjusting.

"For the army, you say? How interesting. Are you working for them now, perhaps?"

"In what way?" Fargo hedged. Distrust had flared on the faces of the others, and Calvin had raised the shotgun.

"The army has been trying its best to get us to leave our new home for months now," Frank Haxton said. "Or should I say trying its worst? The commanding officer at Fort Craig went so far as to threaten to drive us out, but I called his bluff and he backed down. We will not be intimidated by him or anyone else."

Calvin's jaw muscles were twitching and he was fingering the shotgun as if he dearly desired to use it. "So you're Skye Fargo? I've heard a lot about you."

"Have you?"

"From my wife, Danette. You did her and some other ladies a good turn once. To hear her talk, you can walk on water. I sometimes wonder—" Calvin stopped, then said coldly, "I have long wanted to make your acquaintance."

"Pleased to make yours," Fargo said. Whatever Danette had told her husband had fired him with jealously, and jealous men were often violent men. "Glad she finally found the right man to marry."

"Are you indeed? She is the right woman for me, and I intend to stay married to her for a good many years yet." Calvin paused. "Tell me. How well were the two of you acquainted?"

Tricia saved Fargo from having to answer by putting her hands on her father's shoulders and asking, "Should we be standing around like this with Ojo Blanco and a war party after Skye and me?"

"What's that?" Haxton said. "They're chasing you? Perfect! There is nothing I would like more than to send that heathen to hell."

"But there are twenty Apaches and only four of you."

75

One of the farmers patted his Henry. "Don't you fret, missy. With these we can hold off a hundred savages."

Stupidity never impressed Fargo. "On open ground, maybe," he said, and gestured at the boulders littering the slope, "but here your repeating rifles won't help much."

The farmer regarded him with scorn. "Shows how much you know, sonny. We drove those vermin off before. They've been afraid of us ever since."

Fargo almost laughed in his face. Apaches were many things. They were devious. They were bold. They were arrogant. They were violent. But no one in his right mind would ever accuse Apaches of cowardice. "Keep on believing that and you'll be dead before the year is out."

The farmer was disposed to argue, but Frank Haxton held up his hand. "We can discuss this later. Right now let's take my daughter to my wife, then we'll decide how to go about rescuing Lucy."

"My poor child," Elias said forlornly. "What if I never set eyes on her again? I couldn't bear it."

"We will not give up so long as I draw breath," Haxton vowed. He crooked a finger at Tricia and Fargo. "Bring your horses. Ours are just over the ridge."

Calvin Peters brought up the rear, and Fargo swore he could feel the man's eyes bore into his back. As if he did not have enough to deal with, now he had a vengeful husband on his hands. They came to where the farmers' mounts were hidden, and everyone climbed on and headed south. Calvin Peters again made it a point to be last. Fargo did not like having the man behind him, but there was nothing he could do about it for the time being.

Frank Haxton was in the lead, Tricia beside him. Fargo gigged the Ovaro up to join them. "Mind if we talk?"

"You don't beat around the bush, do you?" was Haxton's rejoinder.

"Which bush would that be?"

Haxton stared at him with an air of irritation. "Oh, come now. I'm not stupid. You have admitted you work for the army."

Fargo had not admitted any such thing but he said nothing.

"As I told you, Major Marshall has been trying for months to force us out of our valley. First he suggested we leave in our own best interests. Then he made a formal request. When that failed, he ordered us out, but he knows as well as I do that he does not have the authority to make his order stick. At our last meeting, he practically begged me, claiming he was only thinking of the women and the children." Haxton laughed. "He doesn't understand. He never has. I refused, yet again, and he turned ugly. He pounded his desk and told me that he would find a way to evict us, by hook or by crook. His very words." Haxton grinned at Fargo. "Are you his hook or his crook?"

Fargo had to hand it to him. Haxton was shrewd. Since denying it would be pointless, he responded, "The major did ask me to look into it. But he really is concerned about your welfare."

"Oh, please. The only thing Major Marshall is concerned about is his career. It would not look good on his record if we are massacred. The army, after all, is supposed to protect us."

Tricia said, "I've met the major, Father. He strikes me as being a decent man. As for protecting you, you're asking the impossible."

"My dear daughter," Haxton said smugly, "I am not asking anything of the army, now or ever. We do not want their help. We do not need their help. We are perfectly able to protect ourselves."

"Seventeen farmers and their families against hundreds of Mimbre Apaches," Fargo said. "You don't stand a prayer."

"That's where you're wrong. Prayer will be our salvation. We have put our complete trust in the Lord."

"To Apaches that means less than nothing," Fargo said bluntly.

"Ah. But to the faithful it means everything. Just as our Maker delivered the Israelites from the wilderness, so will our Maker deliver us from the heathens and sustain us in our new home." Haxton spoke with the tone of someone who was completely and totally sure of himself.

"Does mother feel the same way you do?" Tricia asked.

"Your mother always does as I want. You know that."

"But what are her personal feelings? Does she like Paradise Valley as much as you do?"

"It is the promised land," Frank Haxton declared.

"It is Mimbre land," Fargo said, "and when they are ready, they will wipe you out and burn your farms, and the valley will be theirs again."

"You give them too much credit."

"And you don't give them enough," Fargo countered. "The major told me you had a clash with them and won, thanks to your Henrys. But you took them by surprise. Next time, it will be different."

"You sound just like the major," Haxton said harshly, "and I will tell you the same thing I told him. Do not waste my time, and yours, in a fruitless bid to persuade us to leave. We are here to stay."

Fargo fell silent. He had yet to reach Paradise Valley and it seemed that already he had failed. Haxton was right about one thing; there was no talking to him. No getting the man to admit he was wrong. Because Haxton was never wrong. He was one of those who would never admit to a mistake.

Fargo had met people like him before. They had traits in common; they were pigheaded, they seldom gave any thought to others. Look at Haxton; he thought only of himself, and his dream, and was blind to the peril he had placed his followers in.

No, if Fargo was to save them, it would not be through Frank Haxton. He must find another way.

Hours passed. The landscape was as dry and bleak as ever, broken only by scattered pockets of brown vegetation.

It was Frank Haxton who broke the long silence by turning to his daughter and saying out of the blue, "You need a new husband."

Startled, Patricia blurted, "What?"

"You heard me. I have been pondering. It would be remiss of me to let you make a fool of yourself twice. Your mother and I warned you that your first husband was shiftless, but you wouldn't listen."

"Must you keep bringing that up?" Tricia was stung. "I was wrong. I admit it. What more do you want?"

"I want you to be happy," Haxton said, "which is why I will pick your new husband myself."

"I am a grown woman. I have the right to choose my own."

"His name is Merrill. He is Elias's son. He is two years older than you and a fine, strapping young man. It is a wonderful match, if I do say so myself."

"Father, please."

Frank Haxton was not even looking at her. "You need a good man, a decent man, a man who will not run off on you. Someone who gives more than lip service to the Almighty." He paused. "Someone like me."

"But I've never met this Merrill. I might not like him."

"Love is like a seed, daughter. Plant it in good soil, water it, nurture it, and it will grow. Get to know Merrill and you will grow to love him, and you will thank me for my wisdom."

Fargo remembered Tricia grabbing Ojo Blanco's rifle to save him, and remarked, "It must be nice to be better than everyone else."

"I beg your pardon?" Haxton shifted in his saddle. "You have no say in this. It is a family matter between my daughter and me."

"Some father you are," Fargo said. "She came all this way to see you and you want to marry her off against her will."

"That will be quite enough out of you."

Fargo was about to give Haxton a taste of saloon language when Calvin Peters gave a holler.

"Frank! Look yonder! Can that be what I think it is?"

They all drew rein and turned in the saddle. To the north, dust rose toward the blue vault of sky. Dust stirred by a large number of riders.

"Apaches!" one of the farmers declared.

"It's Ojo Blanco, I bet," Tricia said. "I warned you he was after us."

"Stick with me," Fargo told her, and brought the Ovaro to a gallop, heading to the southwest and a slope split by a ravine. A glance assured him she was following. Her father and the other farmers had hesitated, the farmers looking to Frank Haxton to tell them what to do. If they wanted to make their stand there, they were welcome to. They might repel the first rush, maybe even the second. But there were not enough of them to hold off twenty Apaches forever. Fargo would make his stand in the ravine. It offered protection, however slight.

A second glance showed Haxton and the farmers racing to catch up. Haxton did not look happy.

Fargo shucked his Henry from the saddle scabbard and jacked the trigger guard to lever a round into the chamber. He rode into the ravine and came to a stop in a swirling cloud of dust. Vaulting down, he scrambled up the slightly inclined side to the top, and lay flat.

The dust to the north was thicker. Under it were stick figures.

"How soon do you reckon?" Tricia asked, plopping at his side.

"Five minutes," Fargo estimated.

"Don't let them take me. If it comes to that, do what you have to or give me a gun and I will."

The ravine resounded to the clatter of the farmers' mounts. Frank Haxton lost no time in climbing to their vantage point. He did not take cover. He stood exposed from the waist up, his Henry casually cradled in his left arm. "The next time, Mr. Fargo, I will decide our course of action. Is that clear?"

"If there is one," Fargo said.

"For someone who must deal with Indians a lot, you have a remarkably high opinion of them."

"For someone who doesn't know the first thing about them," Fargo mimicked him, "you have a remarkably low opinion."

"Indians are Nature's two-legged rats. Shoot them in the right spot and they die the same as everything else."

"Rats don't shoot back."

Calvin, Elias, and the third farmer were taking up positions across the opening, their Henrys gleaming like drawn swords.

"You are about to observe something that will fill you with pride, daughter," Haxton said to Tricia. "The natural superiority of the white man over the red, put to the ultimate test."

"We are not any better than they are," Tricia said.

Haxton tore his gaze from the Apaches. "Where do you come up with these notions of yours? Do Indians have steam engines? Do they cross the ocean in huge ships? Do they have the telescope? The microscope? Do they have the printing press? The sewing machine?" Her father shook his head. "No, the white man is naturally superior to the red in every regard."

"I never realized how big a bigot you arc, Father."

Haxton recoiled. "I am glad your mother is not here. It would break her heart to hear you talk so."

The stick figures acquired form and substance: Ojo Blanco in all his fury, and the warriors who had been with him. It was rare for them to strike so openly. Apaches were masters of the ambush. They had a thousand and one inventive ways to sneak in on an enemy and dispatch that enemy with ridiculous ease. But for Ojo Blanco, Fargo knew, this had become personal. Fargo had struck him, had knocked him unconscious. It was an insult. An Apache must never let an enemy best him. More so an Apache leader.

"Behold the craven nature of the red race," Frank Haxton said to Tricia, and fired a shot at the war party, even though they were too far off. But if he thought a single shot would send the Mimbres scurrying, he was wrong, as wrong as he was about so much else.

The war party kept coming.

"Don't worry," Haxton said. "Once we have dropped a few of them the rest will turn tail."

"Care to bet?" Fargo asked.

The Mimbres were slowing. They were still out of rifle range. Ojo Blanco veered to the east and the rest followed. He circled the ravine, the stock of his rifle on his thigh.

Fargo imagined the hatred glittering in Ojo Blanco's dark eyes. Ojo Blanco hated whites as much as Frank Haxton hated the red man. They were a lot alike, these two, but would never admit it. The gulf of mutual loathing was too vast.

Tricia raised herself on her elbows. "What will they do? Wait until dark and crawl in close?"

Her father chuckled. "They are welcome to try." He wedged his Henry to his shoulder, pulled back the hammer, spent a minute taking precise aim, and fired.

The slug kicked up dirt fifty yards short of the Apaches.

"Save your ammo," Fargo said.

"It's mine to do with as I please," Haxton testily replied. "And for your information, each of us carries a hundred rounds in our saddlebags. That makes four hundred cartridges, and only twenty-one savages. I'd say we have ammo to spare."

The Apaches stopped circling. Ojo Blanco turned his horse so it was broadside to the ravine and raised his rifle. Fargo had glimpsed it earlier—a single-shot Sharps. "Get down," he said to Tricia, and ducked his head below the rim.

Haxton thought it funny. "The great scout, afraid of a miserable redskin. If I can't hit him, he can't hit us."

No sooner were the words out of his mouth than the Sharps boomed like distant thunder and an earthen geyser erupted not two feet in front of Haxton. The speed with which he dropped flat was a tribute to his reflexes.

Fargo chuckled. "You were saying?" Taking off his hat, he raised his eyes to the top.

Ojo Blanco had resumed circling. One of the warriors, though, stayed where he was, turning his mount so it faced the ravine. Soon a second did the same, then a third, each about the same distance from the other.

"They're surrounding us," Tricia said. "I was right, wasn't I? As soon as the sun sets they'll sneak in close. We're goners."

"Quit exaggerating. I have the situation well in hand. We are in little danger, if any."

Fargo wanted to punch the man. Only a complete fool couldn't see that Ojo Blanco had them right where he wanted them, and he did not know the meaning of mercy.

8

Were it not for Tricia, Fargo would gladly climb on the Ovaro and ride hell-bent for leather, leaving her father and the rest of the farmers to face the war party on their own. He had never liked bigots, and her father was one of the worst he had ever come across. To Frank Haxton, anyone with red skin was a pile of horse droppings. Even worse, Haxton had an exaggerated opinion of himself. Haxton thought that since the farmers had driven the Apaches off once, it would be ridiculously easy to do it again.

But Fargo had to stay put and watch as the Mimbres formed a living fence around the ravine. Spaced roughly equal distances apart, their rifles or other weapons in hand, they sat and waited with the tireless patience of their kind for the whites to try something, or for a signal from Ojo Blanco to attack, whichever came first.

For Ojo Blanco's part, he was smiling, no doubt in anticipation of the white blood he intended to soon spill.

"What do we do?" Tricia worriedly asked.

"Bide our time," Fargo said, "and when a chance comes, take it."

Frank Haxton sneered in contempt. "You can lie here if you want. But I'm going to charge them. They'll scatter to the four winds and we can ride on to Paradise Valley, none the worse for their antics."

"And if they don't scatter?" Fargo brought up.

"For a scout you sure know precious little about Indians," Haxton insulted him yet again. "Their craven natures compel them to flee when their lives are in peril. As I shall shortly demonstrate."

"That's just not true, Father," Tricia said. "And why are you treating Fargo so rudely? He's only trying to help us."

"We don't need his help, daughter," her father responded. "The Lord is our shield and our strength. We will smite these heathens like Samson smote the Philistines, and in so doing, glorify our Maker." Turning, he slid down the slope to his companions. After a brief exchange, the four mounted their horses.

"Care to join us, Mr. High-and-Mighty?" Calvin Peters called up to Fargo.

"I'm not hankering to get myself killed." That was only one of Fargo's reasons. The other was that he would not put it past Peters to shoot him in the back over Danette. By accident, of course.

"I didn't think you would," Calvin said, dripping spite. "You're one of those who talks real big, but when you are put to the test, you show the true shade of your backbone."

"I'll remember you said that."

Frank Haxton rode to the opening, and paused. Right away, one of the Apaches shouted and the warriors on that side of the ravine moved closer. Ojo Blanco, who was to the west, began to trot around toward the opening.

Haxton fed a cartridge into his Henry, saying, "Are you ready, brothers? Let's show these savages the error of tangling with their betters!" He threw back his head and whooped with glee, and the others joined in. Then, two abreast, they swept out of the ravine and bore down on the nearest Apaches, the two in the lead, Haxton and Calvin, firing on the fly.

Apaches were not stupid. They did not throw their lives away. Kill without being killed was their philosophy. The warriors Haxton and company were charging toward wheeled their mounts and fled.

Predictably, Haxton took that as a sign of weakness. He cackled and banged off more shots.

Tricia gasped. "Look at what the others are doing!"

Fully half the warriors, Ojo Blanco among them, were converging on the farmers from the rear. Intent on the few who had fled, none of the whites noticed the threat behind them.

Half rising, Tricia clutched at Fargo's arm. "We must do something! We can't let them be slaughtered."

Fargo could. Haxton's group had brought it on themselves. But he threw his Henry to his shoulder, centered the sights on a warrior sweeping in from the north, and smoothly stroked the trigger. The warrior's arm flung wide and the Mimbre pitched from his horse headfirst.

"Do it again!" Tricia squealed.

Fargo would have liked to, but the Apaches nearest him had pulled a Comanche trick; they had swung onto the other side of their mounts and were clinging by an arm and an ankle. Hitting one would take more luck than skill, and be nearly impossible to do without wounding the horse. He tried anyway. He sighted on a brawny elbow and elevated the barrel a fraction to compensate for the distance. Mentally crossing his fingers, he fired. The elbow dissolved in a shower of blood, flesh, and bone. The Apache grabbed at his mount's mane but his arm was next to useless. Tumbling onto his shoulder, he rolled over a dozen feet, then pushed up into a crouch, using his good arm. He had dropped his rifle and he lunged for it, his eyes on the rim, and on Fargo, who rose higher for a better shot.

Was it Fargo's imagination, or did their eyes meet? He would swear the Mimbre's mouth curled in a feral snarl. Then he fired, and it was as if an invisible mule delivered an invisible kick to the Apache's chest.

Calvin Peters was the first of the farmers to wonder who was shooting, and to look back. He hollered at Frank Haxton. The farmers came to a stop and, with the supreme confidence born of ignorance, calmly regarded the approaching Apaches.

"Why don't they head back to us?" Tricia cried. "Why are they just sitting there like that?"

Her answer came in the form of a volley. The farmers did not bother trying to hit the Apaches; they aimed at the horses. Three squealed and whinnied and crashed to the ground in a whirl of legs and tails, spilling Mimbres. Exactly as Haxton and his friends counted on. Spurring their mounts, they made for the Apaches who were now on foot.

That was when the other Mimbres brought their own rifles to bear. Their rifles were only single-shot, but there were enough of them and they were close enough that their volley was more lethal; Elias and the fourth farmer were shot, and Frank Haxton's horse buckled under him and toppled onto its side.

Fargo fired to cover them, but now every last Mimbre was racing wide around the ravine. He could not drop them all.

Haxton was on his feet. Calvin Peters reached down to swing him up, and a slug sent Peters's hat flying. More peppered the earth around his prancing horse. Calvin only had Haxton half on when he smacked his legs against his claybank and galloped madly for the ravine. Elias followed, swaying in the saddle.

A Mimbre angled to intercept them.

"They don't see him!" Tricia cried.

Fargo did. The Henry boomed and bucked. The warrior clasped a hand to his shoulder and doubled over. Fargo aimed at another Apache, but the rest had learned and were reining out of range.

Tricia whirled and bounded to the bottom of the ravine, slipping and sliding and nearly falling. Heedless of taking a stray bullet, she ran to the opening. "Hurry! Just a little bit farther!" she shouted.

Her father was hanging from Calvin's saddle, his knees bent so his boots would not scrape. They were almost to the ravine when Calvin's horse dived at the dirt as if the ground were a lake. Calvin and Haxton had no time to throw themselves clear. Haxton was instantly erect, but Calvin did not move.

"We must help them!" Tricia wailed, and ran into the open, her long hair flying, her dress swirling about her legs.

Fargo raced along the rim but stopped when he saw

the Mimbres were gathering their dead and wounded, and withdrawing. Apaches never left their dead behind if they could help it. He had a clear shot at a pair who had a wounded warrior slung between them, but he did not take it. He let them go.

Calvin Peters was either unconscious or dead. Haxton and Tricia struggled mightily to hold him up, Tricia nearly buckling under the heavy weight. Elias and the fourth farmer lay out on the flat, unmoving.

Fargo started down the ravine to help them.

Glancing up, Frank Haxton snapped, "Are you sure it's not too much of an imposition for you to help us?" He stared, openmouthed, as Fargo went past them, to Elias's horse. Snagging the reins, he led the animal back. He overtook them before they reached the ravine.

"The Apaches will pay for this," Haxton was saying to his daughter. "Mark my words. I will see every one of those savages dead."

"There are too many," Tricia said. "You can't fight the entire Apache nation. It just can't be done."

Her know-everything father said, "The Mimbres are not a nation, they are a band. There can't be more than a couple of hundred, if that."

As usual, Frank Haxton was wrong. Fargo happened to know there were three hundred warriors alone, plus the women and children. If all the warriors gathered for an attack on Paradise Valley, the settlers would be wiped out, Henrys or no Henrys. It was rare, though, for that many to undertake an enterprise. Usually they roamed wide and far in small groups, like Ojo Blanco's.

The Mimbres, the Mescaleros, the Chiricahuas and the rest were all fiercely independent. Warriors did as they wanted when they wanted, which made it that much harder for Apaches to wage war as a unified fighting force. There was talk that Mangas Colorado was trying to forge an alliance of all the Apaches and the Navajos to drive the whites out of their country once and for all and forever, but so far the alliance had not come to be. If it did, New Mexico Territory and adjacent regions would become killing grounds.

Tricia and her father placed Calvin Peters on his back, and Tricia examined him. "I can't find a wound."

"He hit his head when his horse threw him," Frank Haxton said. "He's blacked out, is all."

Switching her fingers to Peters's hair, Tricia probed gently. "He has a nasty bump the size of a hen's egg."

Fargo stepped to the Ovaro, and the water skin. "Use some of this." Frank Haxton reached for it, but Fargo gave it to Tricia. "As little as you can. We might be stuck here a while."

"I must say," Frank Haxton declared, "that I find you grate on my kindly nature most severely."

"Is that how you think of yourself?" Fargo shook his head and started up the side of the ravine to check on the Mimbres. He paused when Haxton said his name.

"Why do you bait me so? What have I ever done to you that you detest me like you do? And don't deny it. I see the loathing in your eyes, and in your expression. You detest me and I demand to know why."

"You just got two of your friends killed," Fargo said, "and before this is done, a lot more of your people might die."

"So? What nonsense are you spouting? I wasn't the one who killed Elias and Andrew. The Apaches did."

It never ceased to amaze Fargo how some people couldn't see the truth if it jumped up and bit them on the ass. "Elias and Andrew would not have been here if it were not for you. The same with everyone else at Paradise Valley. Whatever happens from here on out is on your shoulders."

"I'm to be blamed for following my dream? For wanting to establish a God-fearing community where men and women can live in peace and harmony?"

"No, not for the dream," Fargo said, "but for picking *Apache* country!" Another thing that never ceased to amaze him was how many people were running around without brains.

"What is so wrong about that? White men have been pushing into Indian land since the Mayflower landed. Even as we speak, new settlements are springing up west of Denver in Ute country and on Sioux land up north. I am doing no different than untold others have done."

"Indians have a right to be left to live in peace," Fargo said.

"Ah. So you are one of those. An Indian lover. But you are wrong on two counts. First, the United States has laid claim to all the land between the Atlantic and the Pacific. Haven't you heard of Manifest Destiny? It is our right to take land from the heathens and claim it as our own."

Fargo felt himself simmer.

"Second, Indians have no rights. They are not Americans. They are little more than beasts, with simple minds and simple ways. They are inferior to us in every regard, and as such, deserve to be displaced."

"You have it all worked out."

"I am not alone in my sentiments. Have you read the newspapers? Heard our politicians? I daresay most Americans feel as I do. I take it you have heard an expression that has become quite widely used these days?" Frank Haxton grinned. "The only good Indian is a dead Indian."

"I've heard another expression. A parson told it to me once. It's from that Bible you wave around as if you wrote it. Maybe you have heard of it." Fargo paused. "As you reap, so shall you sow."

"Will wonders never cease," Frank Haxton taunted. "A quote from Scripture from the likes of you!"

Tricia interjected, "Father, please. Can't you be civil?"

"I treat the ungodly as they deserve to be treated, daughter." Haxton jabbed a finger at Fargo. "I have heard of this friend of yours. They say he is a flagrant womanizer who spends all his spare time in dens of iniquity." He glared at Fargo. "I defy you to deny it."

"Why deny the truth?" Fargo retorted.

"There? You see?" Haxton crowed to Tricia. "He admits his reprobate nature. He is a sinner and we should have no truck with him."

"It doesn't count that I'm white?" Fargo asked.

"Again you mock me," Haxton responded. "In truth, there is no difference between you and the Apaches. You are as ungodly as they are."

"Thank you," Fargo said, and resumed climbing.

"For what?"

"Saying I'm more like an Apache than you." Fargo did not glance down to see if his joust had scored. He continued to the top and lay flat. He did not see a single Mimbre, living or dead. They had vanished. Whether they were gone for good or had gone off to lick their wounds was anyone's guess.

Gravel clattered, and Patricia deposited herself next to him, her arm brushing his. "I'm sorry about how he treats you."

"You don't have anything to do with it," Fargo said. "You have nothing to apologize for."

"He's my father," Tricia said, as if that alone were enough.

"He's a jackass."

Tricia tittered, then covered her mouth as if embarrassed. "I'm not a dutiful daughter, am I? To think so poorly of my own parent."

"You think for yourself. That's more important."

"I thought so, once," Tricia said softly. "Then I went and made the mistake of marrying a man I never should have married. It made me realize I'm no smarter than my father. I have no right judging him."

"You can't let him browbeat you, either," Fargo said. "There are times in our lives when we have to stand on our own two feet."

Tricia placed her hand on his. "But we are who we are, and I happen to be his daughter. I can't cut the string, no matter how dearly I might want to."

"It might get you killed," Fargo observed.

"Not if we can get him to leave Paradise Valley. Maybe that woman the major mentioned can help. Your friend, Danette Peters."

Fargo did not see how. The other farmers were loyal to Frank Haxton. They believed in him, or they would not have followed him into the heart of Apache territory.

Paradise Valley was its own little kingdom, and Haxton was their king. What could Danette say or do to convince them they were wrong?

"Life can be so complicated," Tricia remarked. "Why couldn't my father have stayed in the East where we belong?"

"For some the grass is always greener in the next pasture," Fargo said. But he was a fine one to talk. He never could stay in one place very long.

"If we can't persuade my parents to leave," Tricia said, "I will sever all ties with them. I will go off on my own and make a go of it somewhere else. Saint Louis, perhaps, or New Orleans. There are more jobs for women to be had in bigger cities. I'll find an apartment and—" Tricia stopped, and gasped.

Fargo twisted. She was looking down. He followed her gaze, and simmered anew. Instantly he was up and bounding to the bottom, saying, "I told you to go easy with that."

Frank Haxton had the water skin tilted to his mouth and was guzzling water as if they had an unlimited supply. Excess spilled over his chin and dampened the front of his shirt. Lowering it, he let out a contented sigh. "I was thirsty, so I helped myself."

"That water has to last."

"There is plenty at Paradise Valley, and we will be there in a day or two." Haxton raised the water skin toward his lips again.

"Don't," Fargo warned.

Haxton sneered at him. "I have had just about enough of your attitude. I will do as I damn well please and there is nothing you can do about it."

"Think so?" Fargo said, and planted his fist in Frank Haxton's stomach. He did not use all his strength, but enough that Haxton folded to his knees, wheezing and sputtering, and the water skin fell from fingers suddenly gone limp. Fargo caught it before it struck the ground. "Don't touch this again unless you ask." He carried the water skin to the Ovaro and slung it over his saddle.

"Skye! Look out!"

Fargo heard the rush of footsteps and tried to skip aside, but hands seized the back of his buckskin shirt and he was whirled around and propelled toward a waist-high boulder. He put his hands out to cushion the impact, and had to let go of the Henry. It clattered at his feet as pain shot up both arms and into his shoulders. A blow low in the back caused the sky and the earth to spin and bright pinpoints to flare before his eyes.

"Ask your permission?" Frank Haxton said shrilly. "Who do you think you are, telling *me* what to do?"

Another blow, to the temple, nearly caved Fargo's legs out from under him. Sidestepping, he shook his head to clear it.

"I have put up with all I intend to from you!" Haxton roared. "I am going to pound you to a pulp and send you back to that uppity major as a warning to leave us be."

The world stopped spinning. Fargo set himself and raised both fists. "Not very Biblical of you."

About to wade in, Frank Haxton scowled. "There you go again. Throwing my faith in my face. But who are you to judge me? You cavort with loose women, you gamble, you drink."

"Your point?" Fargo asked, and as he spoke, he swung. His knuckles connected solidly with Haxton's jaw and the farmer staggered, but almost immediately recovered and stood there rubbing his chin and eyeing Fargo with his hatred increased tenfold.

"You are stronger than you look, but it doesn't matter. I will make an example of you."

"You'll try," Fargo said. He had listened to enough. He was on Haxton before the other could blink, unleashing a whirlwind of punches, intending to end it quickly. He almost succeeded. He caught Haxton on the ribs, and Haxton snapped forward into an uppercut that by rights should have stretched him out like a board. But for all Haxton's faults, a glass jaw was not one of them. He retaliated in kind, his big fists flashing in staccato cadence.

Fargo slipped a right, blocked a left, delivered a flurry

that stung his hands and rocked Haxton, but the man was made of iron and would not go down. He ducked a straight-arm from the shoulder and nearly had his teeth caved in by Haxton's knee. But he could fight dirty, too. He smashed his boot down on the toes of Haxton's left foot, and when Haxton swore lustily and involuntarily glanced down, Fargo followed through with another uppercut. Only this time he put all his weight and every sinew in his body into it, his fist streaking up from near his shin and shooting for the clouds.

The *crack* of knuckles on bone was like the crack of a gunshot. Haxton tottered and blinked and feebly swung, but he had to be seeing double because his fist came nowhere near Fargo.

"Had enough?"

"Go to hell."

Fargo cocked his fist to finish it.

Suddenly, Patricia was between them, pushing her father back, tears dampening her cheeks. "Please! Stop this! For my sake!"

Frank Haxton sought to push her away, but she held her ground. "Move aside, girl! I heard you warn him! My own flesh and blood, and you betrayed me."

"Don't be foolish."

Her father lowered his arms and regarded her as if she had just crawled out from under a rock. "So now I'm a fool, am I, on top of everything else?"

Tricia reached for his hand but he jerked back. "Please don't put words in my mouth. I love you, Father. I always have."

"You love me so much, you married that no-account against my wishes. You love me so much, the two of you ran off and left me to deal with your mother's tears and sleepless nights." Haxton raised a hand to strike her, but lowered it without doing so. "If you ask me, you only love us when it suits you. The rest of the time you can't be bothered." Wheeling, he walked off.

"Please," Tricia pleaded, and uttered a low sob, "don't do this."

Fargo felt sorry for her, but there was nothing he could do. She turned and ran past him to be by herself.

"What's going on? What did I miss?" Calvin Peters had sat up and was gingerly rubbing his head. "The last I remember is being shot at by the Apaches. Where are they?"

"That's what I need to find out." Fargo climbed on the Ovaro and gigged the stallion out of the ravine. He passed Frank Haxton, but Haxton did not look at him. There was still no sign of the Mimbres.

Fargo found it hard to accept that Ojo Blanco had given up. Half an hour and a wide circle around the ravine later, he drew rein and scratched his head in puzzlement. They were gone, all right, but that begged the question *why*? What could possibly draw the Mimbres away? An answer rose unbidden, the only answer that made sense, and he shivered in the blistering heat.

9

Paradise Valley was aptly named. It was a shock to crest a sawtooth rise and set eyes on so much green in an unending sea of brown. The stream responsible for the wealth of green flowed year-round, a rarity in that part of the mountains. Lush green grass, belts of green timber—everywhere one gazed, green and more green.

That alone was enough to set the valley apart. But now, thanks to the farmers, it was unique for another reason. For only here in the entire stretch of stark mountains between Albuquerque and the border with Mexico was a sight that made Fargo think he had somehow pierced the veil of distance and ridden into a valley in Illinois or Virginia or Pennsylvania or any of the other verdant states east of the Mississippi River.

Plows had been taken to the rich soil. Crops had been planted. To ensure the corn and oats and wheat withstood the fiery New Mexico sun, irrigation ditches had been dug, a network of blue ribbons that crisscrossed the valley from end to end, laid out in large squares so that the entire valley resembled a giant checkerboard. Farmhouses, barns, and outbuildings added to the feeling that the valley had been transplanted whole from back east. Timber was scarce, so most of the farmhouses were small, the barns not much bigger. The individual plots were arranged so that the buildings were at the center of each fifty-acre allotment.

People were everywhere, moving about: men working in the fields or near their barns, women on their knees in flower gardens or hoeing vegetable gardens or hanging clothes to dry. Young children scampered at play, older children were busy with various chores.

Fargo expected to see the grass and the tilled fields and the buildings. He did not expect to see so many cattle. Over a hundred head in scattered, fenced pastures, perhaps twenty head to a pasture.

At each end of the valley were two special structures. Tall towers, shaped like needles, fifty feet high, with ladders to a roost at the top. From up there, sentries had a clear view of the entire valley and the adjacent slopes.

All in all, Fargo had to reluctantly hand it to Frank Haxton. The settlement was well planned and well run. But it was still a mistake. It was still a disaster waiting to happen.

"Well, well, well," Haxton said with a heavy dollop of sarcasm. "Where are the Apaches? You had us ride like the dickens to get here. We about wore ourselves out, and all because you had a hunch the Mimbres were going to overrun our homesteads. Yet look. Everything is exactly as it should be."

"I thought for sure Ojo Blanco would come here," Fargo said. He had envisioned arriving too late to prevent a massacre.

"Which goes to show you really don't know any more about Indians than we do," Haxton gloated. "Yet you're supposed to be an expert."

"Stop it," Tricia said. "Stop treating him as if he's dirt."

Her father's lip curled in disdain. "There you go again. Siding with him against me. Why you bothered to come, I will never know."

Tricia was riding double with him. "I wanted to see mother and you. Believe it or not, I do love you."

"The proof is in the pudding, daughter, and when you ran off with that shiftless excuse for a husband, you proved that you don't love us as much as you claim. If you did, if you truly and really cared, you would do as we say to do and not take it into your head to live contrary to our wishes."

"Let's not go through this again, shall we?"

At that moment several loud, tinny blasts came from the tower at the near end of the valley. Blasts from a trumpet, if Fargo was not mistaken; three long notes and a short note. At the signal, nearly everyone within sight stopped what they were doing and turned toward the rise.

"How did they know where we are?" Tricia wondered.

"Look at the tower," Haxton said.

Fargo did, and saw the sentry was standing for all to see, holding his rifle at arm's length, pointing straight at them.

"The towers were my idea," Frank Haxton boasted. "The Apaches can't possibly sneak up on us."

"During the day, maybe," Fargo said. "But what about at night?"

"Apaches rarely attack after dark. You should know that." Haxton snickered. "But if they did, they would be in for a surprise."

Fargo started down. He was riding double with Calvin Peters, who had not said four words the entire time.

The inhabitants of Paradise Valley hurried to meet them, men, women, and children—some on horseback, some on foot.

"Head for the tower, if you would," Frank Haxton requested with mock politeness. "I must speak to my people."

Fargo had noticed that Haxton had a habit of calling the other settlers "his." As if Haxton owned them.

"There's mother!" Tricia exclaimed in delight, and broke into a trot to reach the tower that much sooner.

About to do the same, Fargo felt Calvin Peters's steely fingers clamp on to his shoulder.

"I'll say this once and only once, mister. Stay away from my wife. She speaks too highly of you for my liking."

"We're friends," Fargo said.

"I wouldn't care if you were cousins," Calvin rumbled. "I keep a tight rein on her, you understand? I don't like other men being around her. That goes double for someone like you."

Fargo checked a sharp retort. For the time being, he would do his best to get along. He must keep thinking of all the women and children who stood to end up in early graves if he did not succeed.

"I mean it." Calvin would not let it rest, as if he sensed the threat was not being taken seriously. "If I catch you anywhere near her, there will be hell to pay. I'm not Frank. I'm bigger than he is, and meaner than he is, and when I lay into you, you'll wish you hadn't been born."

Many of the mounted settlers had reached the north tower. Frank Haxton climbed down and was warmly greeted, with a lot of smiles and back clapping.

A small woman with limp brown hair came out of the crowd and halted a few feet from Tricia. They stared at one another uncertainly, the daughter unsure of her reception, the mother as timid as a mouse. Then Tricia sobbed and threw her arms wide and her mother walked into them and they stood in silent embrace, tears glistening on both faces.

Calvin Peters went over to stand beside Frank Haxton.

Left by himself, Fargo stayed well back. A lot of stares were thrown in his direction, some merely curious, most openly unfriendly. The good people of Paradise Valley did not readily take to strangers.

Then a pretty woman in a calico dress, her hair down past her shoulders, happily skipped toward him, declaring, "I knew you would come! I just knew it!" She practically threw herself at him and clung to him as if she were drowning and he was a log she had to hold on to for dear life. "Skye," she said softly. "Oh, Skye."

"How have you been, Danette?"

The former Danette Landry smiled warmly, her hands on his hips. She appeared the same except around the eyes, where she now had lines that were not there before. She also had an air of weariness about her. Not physical fatigue, but deeper weariness, the kind that suggested that deep down inside she was tired of life and her part in it. "I've been getting by."

"It's good to see you," Fargo said. "Major Marshall told me that it was your idea to send for me."

Danette gave a start and glanced over her shoulder. "Keep your voice down, please! The others will tar and feather me if they find out."

"You're only trying to prevent a bloodbath."

"They wouldn't see it that way. To them it would be a betrayal of everything they believe in." Danette clasped his hands. "Can't we talk about something else? It's been so long."

There were a few things Fargo wanted to sort out first. "The major says you think I can be of help somehow."

"There's that, yes." Danette hesitated. "But it's only part of the reason."

"What's the other part?"

"We can't talk here. Later. I'll find a way to meet you somehow." Danette squeezed his fingers. "I've told my husband about you. Well, some of it, anyway. If I told him everything, he would beat me."

"Weren't you supposed to marry a prospector?" Fargo recollected. "How did you end up with Calvin Peters?"

"I'd never met that prospector, remember?" Danette reminded him. "All we did was share letters through the matrimonial bureau. He wrote such sweet ones. But every word in them was a lie. He did not look like he said he looked. He was twenty years older than he claimed to be. And he had the most godawful teeth. Teeth so rotten, you couldn't stand to be close to him for his breath."

"So you turned him down?"

"I had that right," Danette said. "It was in my contract with the bureau. They tried to get me interested in some-one else, but I'd had enough of their shenanigans. I went back east, to the small town where I was born and raised. That's where I ran into Calvin."

Fargo folded his arms. "You let him court you?"

"What can I say?" Danette shrugged. "I wasn't getting any younger, and I didn't care to live my life a spinster. Cal was rough around the edges, but he had a place of his own and the healthiest teeth you ever did see. So, yes, I let him court me. One thing led to another, and he asked me to marry him."

"It was his idea to come here?"

"How did you guess? I'd had enough of the frontier. I wanted to stay where it was safe. But Calvin wouldn't listen. Haxton had filled his head with notions of a virtual paradise, ours for the taking. A land of milk and honey, Haxton called it. Heaven on earth."

"And here you are." Fargo saw that Frank Haxton was climbing the ladder to the tower.

"Here I am," Danette said with disgust. "Stuck in the middle of a war I want no part of. Stuck in a territory I never wanted to visit. And stuck with a man whose middle name is Stubborn with a capital S."

"You can always leave him."

"And do what? Work in saloons? I'd rather not. Divorced women are preyed on like lambs by every wolf in pants."

Haxton was almost to the top of the tower. The sentry gave him a hand onto the platform, and Haxton rose and stared down at the scores of upturned faces. "Brothers and sisters, may I have your attention?" He raised his arms for silence. "I bear tidings. Unwelcome tidings. Brace yourselves."

"Where is my Andrew?" a woman shouted.

"Did you find any trace of my daughter Lucy?" a woman hollered. "Please tell me you did!"

Frank Haxton had a flair for theatrics. Bowing his head, he intoned solemnly, "That is the first of my bad tidings. No, we did not come across so much as a trace of your pride and joy. Your husband refused to give up, though. We would still be searching if we had not run into Ojo Blanco."

At mention of the Mimbre, a general murmur spread.

"The second bad tiding is that we have lost two of our beloved brethren. Andrew and Elias have gone on to their rewards."

Andrew's wife let out a scream. Other women sought to comfort her while the rest waited uneasily for more shocking revelations.

"My third bad tiding is *him*," Frank Haxton declared, and pointed at Fargo. "He is a scout for the army. The government sent him to find a way to force us to leave our homes."

Another, louder, murmur spread like wildfire.

Danette glanced sharply at Fargo. "Dear God. How did he find that out? I did my best to keep my meetings with Major Marshall a secret." She seemed to shrivel in upon herself. "I'm in for it now. They will punish me. Wait and see."

Frank Haxton had gone on. "The government will not let us be. We have assured them time and again that we can take care of ourselves, but will they listen? No! We have a legal right to be here, but do they acknowledge that right? Again, no! This land is ours. We will not let anyone, not the government, not the army, not Ojo Blanco or the entire Mimbre tribe, drive us off!"

Cheers of agreement went up.

"We are with you, Brother Haxton!"

"A pox on the army!"

"We are here to stay!"

A stocky farmer jabbed a thick thumb at Fargo and barked, "I say we send the scout packing! We don't want his kind here!"

"I agree!" another man shouted. "Let's tie him down over his horse and give it a smack on the rump!"

More murmuring ensued, and a few of the more excitable started toward Fargo. They stopped at a command from Haxton.

"I share your anger, brothers. But we must always keep Scripture in mind. We must not harm the scout. Instead, we will turn the other cheek. We will permit the government spy to spend the night in our fair community. But come tomorrow, by noon, he must be gone, or suffer our righteous wrath."

Cries of assent arose, and Haxton silenced them with a wave. "For now, we have grieving families to attend to. All of you are invited to my house. I will butcher a cow and we will treat ourselves to a feast fit for Herod. After we eat, we will sit down together and plan how best to deal with the Apaches."

"What can we do that we have not already done?" This from Calvin Peters.

"So far we have been content to stay to ourselves," Haxton responded. "We have endured their thievery. We have suffered their attack, which we repulsed without any loss of life. But now they have taken fair young Lucy, killed her father, Elias, and slain our good friend Andrew. We will endure no more." Haxton straightened and squared his shoulders. "Enough is enough! Our next step is to bait the Apaches in their own lair."

Fargo could not believe what he was hearing. "You're going into the mountains after the Mimbres?" He would not give a wooden coin for their chances, and said so.

"Your opinions hold no merit with us, outsider," was Haxton's response. "You are our enemy, as surely as the Apaches themselves."

"Did you ever think that it's exactly what the Apaches want?" Fargo asked. "That by taking Lucy, they were hoping to draw you out. Hoping to fight you on their terms and not on yours."

Frank Haxton laughed merrily. "You give them more credit than they are due. They're simple savages. Dumb brutes in human guise. To suggest they are capable of a higher plane of thought is silly."

"Someone is dumb as a stump, that's for sure," Fargo said under his breath. Then, louder, so everyone could hear, "For once listen to someone other than your leader. You can't go on like this. You can't ignore the truth."

"And what would that be?" a woman angrily demanded.

"That the Apaches will win."

Hoots and a few insults greeted his statement. An older woman summed up the feelings of the rest by yelling, "May the devil take you and your dire predictions! We had an earful of them from that major! We want you gone, outsider. Tomorrow can't come soon enough to suit us."

They left him there alone by the tower, the sentry

glowering down. Their hatred was a stinging slap to the face. Fargo had never much cared what others thought of him, and he did not much care now, but to be hated by so many was an unsettling experience.

The sole exception was Danette Peters. Before she dutifully followed her hulking husband off across the valley, she rose on the tips of her toes and whispered in Fargo's ear that she would talk to him that night at the Haxton farm.

Fargo looked forward to seeing her. Personally, he was at a loss as to how to save the settlers from their stupidity. As surely as the sun rose and set every day, as surely as the tides washed the continental shores and the stars sparkled at night, they were all going to die unless he came up with a brainstorm. Or Danette did. He was counting on her. She had sent for him. She must have some idea how to go about it.

While he waited for the get-together to start, Fargo rode the length and breadth of Paradise Valley. No one tried to stop him. No one cursed him, or otherwise gave voice to their hatred. But their eyes were on him. He felt their glares, from one farm to the next, and part of him wanted to throw their hatred back in their faces by riding out then and there. It would serve them right if Ojo Blanco did wipe them out.

Then he would see small children at play, and a mother with a baby in her arms, a father petting a dog, a man brushing a horse, and he was reminded that for all their hatreds, they were human beings. They were ordinary people, no more or less pigheaded than most others. The knowledge made their glares a bit easier to bear.

At length, the sun balanced on the western rim of the world, setting the sky ablaze with vivid streaks of red, orange, and yellow. From every farmhouse in the valley came those who had claimed it as their own. Lots were drawn and, before supper began, two men went to relieve the sentries in the north and south towers.

When Fargo rode up nearly everyone was there. Once again he was treated to cold stares and cold shoulders.

He strode among them with his thumbs hooked in his gunbelt, a prowling panther among bulls, cows, and calves. No one spoke to him. No one met his gaze. When he stopped at a table to help himself to an inch-thick slab of beef and a baked potato smothered in butter, those nearest him decided to be less near.

From snatches of conversation Fargo overheard, he knew that Frank Haxton would give another speech once the meal was over. He had been there an hour and most of the farmers were sitting around savoring a rare treat, beer, when perfume wreathed him like a cloud and a hand fell on his shoulder.

"We need to have that talk," Danette Peters said.

"Here?"

"No. Follow me. My husband is over with Frank. We can be by ourselves." Danette reached out to grasp his hand but apparently changed her mind, dropped her arm, and glanced furtively about. "I mustn't forget myself."

The sun had set. Twilight was giving way to the sway of night. Lanterns were lit and hung from pegs or placed on tables.

The barn was dark and quiet. Inside were a plow horse and two cows, standing placidly in their stalls. The smell of fresh-cut hay tingled Fargo's nose as Danette led him into the shadows, to a ladder that would take them to the hayloft.

"Why up there?" Fargo asked.

"We need somewhere private, somewhere they won't think to look for us." Danette placed her hands on a rung.

"Here is fine." The last thing Fargo needed was to be caught up in the loft with the wife of one of the farmers.

"What?" Danette wore her disappointment like a shroud. "It's more comfortable in the loft."

"Here," Fargo insisted, and pulled her over by a stall. Leaning against it, he said, "We don't have a lot of time. The Mimbres will come soon, in force. Maybe not tomorrow or the next day or the day after, but they will. If you have some idea how I can save your friends, I need to hear it."

"Me?" Danette said.

"You asked the major to send for me," Fargo said. "You must have a plan."

Her laugh was a nail in the valley's coffin. "I wanted to see you again, yes. But it has nothing to do with the Mimbres or the fools my husband has sided with. I sent for you for myself. I needed to see you again. To ask you to take me out of here."

Fargo bowed his head.

"I can't stand it another day. I made a mistake marrying Cal. He's not the man I thought he was." Danette stepped closer, her bosom brushing his chest, the fragrance of her perfume stronger than ever. "Save me, please."

"What about the rest?"

"What about them?" Danette retorted. "They will never listen to reason. Major Marshall talked himself silly and it went in Frank Haxton's ear and out the other."

"So I take you and we go, and the Apaches come and wipe out everyone else?" Fargo said.

Danette tilted her head. "If they want to die, let them. They have brought it on themselves. But I don't need to die with them." She studied him. "Why did you ask that? What's gotten into you?"

Fargo looked into her limpid eyes, and had never loathed anyone more. "I could ask the same thing."

"We were close, weren't we?" Danette said. "Only for a few nights, yes, but I think of them a lot. I think of you. You were the best lover I ever had."

It was like a kick to the groin, only worse. Fargo's insides twisted. He had liked her once, a little.

"I know what you are thinking. I can see it on your face. You're thinking I'm selfish. That I only care about myself."

Fargo did not respond.

"Damn you! When did you become so considerate of others? What are these people to you?"

"I'm not married to one of them," Fargo said.

"Damn you! You have no right to judge me. None whatsoever." Danette swung a flat hand but Fargo caught her wrist. "Let go!" She tried to wrench free but he was too strong. "Don't do this! You are my last hope!"

Fargo heard the scrape of footfalls a second before shadows detached themselves from the greater darkness. In the forefront reared Calvin Peters. Two friends flanked him.

"What's this, my dear?" Calvin asked with sugary sweetness. "Is this man abusing you?"

"Cal! I thought you were with Frank."

Peters's teeth were pale spikes in the gloom. "I noticed you were missing and put myself in your shoes." He smacked his right fist into his left palm. "Now why don't you step aside so we can break every bone in this son of a bitch's body?"

10

Light filled the barn. A fourth farmer had entered carrying a lit lantern and now hung it on a peg. Danette was terrified. She darted to her husband and placed her hands on his broad chest.

"Calvin, please! He wasn't abusing me! Let's have no more talk of breaking bones, shall we?"

Calvin Peters's smile was vicious. "But I say he *was* mistreating you, my dear. I heard him with my own ears. I warned him to stay away from you and he wouldn't listen. He must be punished."

The other farmers wore masks of spite-filled agreement.

Danette gripped her husband's shirt. "No, Cal! I beg you! Nothing happened between us! Your jealousy is uncalled for."

"Is it?" Calvin had not taken his glittering eyes off Fargo. "What kind of husband would I be if I did not defend my wife's honor."

"Didn't you hear what I just said? He has not laid a hand on me. My wifely virtue has not been violated."

"Your what?" Calvin said, and his powerful frame shook with silent mirth. "You gave that up long ago, my dear."

Danette gasped and drew back. Her cheeks reddened. She glanced at the other men, at their mocking expressions, and became redder. Her right hand shot up and connected with a loud *smack*.

It had no more effect on Calvin Peters than would the

bite of a flea. "Are you angry with me, sweetheart? Your devoted husband? After I have given you a roof over you head and done all I can to give you a good life?"

Danette was too mad to reply. Shaking with fury, she balled her fists, but did not hit him.

"All I've done, I have done for you," Calvin said. "When I heard of this valley and Frank's grand plans, I wanted to be part of it for your sake. I wanted to give you all I could. Fine land, a fine home, a fine place to live."

"But I have told you time and again I don't want to be here!" Danette cried, her voice quavering.

"Because you are afraid of the Apaches. Yes. I know. But we have withstood them so far and we will go on withstanding them." Calvin touched her cheek. "You really must have more faith in me."

"I do have faith in you, Cal. I always have. But there is such a thing as overstepping ourselves. You should not have listened to Frank's wild schemes. He has blinded you to the truth."

"And what would that be?" Calvin asked. He had temporarily forgotten about Fargo.

"Just because we are white does not make us better than others. Just because we believe in God does not mean God will strike the Apaches dead on our behalf. That's not how it works."

Calvin's features softened, and for a few seconds Fargo thought she had blunted his anger. Then Calvin sadly shook his head and made a clucking sound.

"All this time I thought you were with me—if not in body, at least in heart and soul. And all this time you have had something wrong with you. I never hear the other wives talk like you just did. I never hear them say they have no faith in their Maker, in their husbands, or in Frank." Calvin paused, and now it was he who grew red with rage. "None of the other wives have the gall to send for an old lover to whisk them away from our valley. None of the other wives would ever insult their husbands so."

"Cal, I didn't—"

Peters did not let her finish. Seizing her by the shoulders, he shook her as if she were a rag doll and he wanted to tear it apart. "Enough! No more of your lies! I heard you! You have branded me a fool, woman, in the eyes of my friends! You have made me a mockery!"

"I did no such thing!"

"I will hear no more," Calvin said, and pushed her at the farmer to his left, who in turn sent her stumbling against the man who had brought the lantern. He held fast to her arms and would not let go.

"Don't do this!" Danette pleaded. "I beg you!"

Calvin Peters faced Fargo. "Pathetic, is she not? Now then. Let's you and I settle things." He began rolling up his sleeves, exposing corded muscles from his wrists to his elbows. "Cat got your tongue? You have been awful quiet."

"Nothing I say would change things."

"True. You really should have more respect for married men. Trifling with their wives is bound to get you into trouble." Calvin rolled up the other sleeve. "Something tells me this isn't the first time, but if I teach you a lesson, it might be your last."

Fargo placed his right hand on his Colt. "Think again."

"You would shoot unarmed men?"

Only then did Fargo realize they did not have rifles or revolvers. They did not even have knives.

"Go ahead, if that's the kind of man you are. Murder us. But you will never make it out of Paradise Valley alive. Frank will see to it that you are hung from the nearest tree."

"I don't want to fight you."

Calvin chuckled and raised his knobby fists. "I wouldn't want to fight me, either. I can bust a rail with one punch. Or a man's head."

Fargo tried one last time. "Nothing happened between your wife and me. She only wanted me to take her away from here."

"By away from here you mean away from me," Calvin said. "I push a plow for a living, but I'm not stupid."

One of the other farmers motioned. "Enough talk, Cal. Get this over with before someone comes looking for us."

"Yes, indeed," said another. "My wife would not stand for any of us brawling like saloon riffraff."

"You heard them." Calvin grinned. "No more talk." He closed in, his bulging shoulders hunched.

Fargo came close to jerking his Colt. At the last split second, he dodged the punch Calvin threw and heard it crack against the stall. Most men would have busted their hand, but Calvin turned and plunged after him, unhurt.

"Stop it, Cal! Please!" Danette wailed.

Peters ignored her. He had eyes only for Fargo, eyes aglow with bloodlust, with the craving to pound and smash.

Backpedaling, Fargo glanced right and left. Against most men he would go toe-to-toe, but against Calvin Peters it would be suicide. A person had to know their limits. Peters was a match for any three ordinary men, and Fargo did not fancy being laid up for a month, or crippled.

Peters was smirking. "Scared, are you? The famous Trailsman? Why not stand still and get it over with?"

Fargo bumped against a bin filled with feed. In it was a bucket. In a blur he whirled and scooped the bucket into the feed. "Not another step," he warned.

Calvin Peters snorted with amusement. "What good will that do you?"

"Let's find out." Fargo swung the bucket, hurling the feed at Calvin's face.

Peters threw an arm up but some of the feed got into his eyes and nose. "Damn you!" he growled. Blinking and coughing, he tried to clear his vision.

Two days ago, Fargo had flattened Frank Haxton with an uppercut. He resorted to another uppercut now, putting all he had into the blow. It was like punching an anvil. He thought he had broken his hand. But it was worth the pain if it ended the fight.

Calvin Peters rocked on his heels. He flung his arms

out for balance and tottered a couple of steps. That was all. Setting himself, still blinking, he grinned and rubbed his chin. "Not bad. No one has ever hit me that hard."

Fargo was in trouble. He sidled to the right but the farmer flanking Peters moved to block him. Again Fargo stabbed for his Colt, but he could not bring himself to shoot. He was not a cold-blooded killer. But who said he had to kill? He palmed the Colt, holding it down low.

Calvin Peters had started toward him, but stopped. "So you are yellow, just like I reckoned."

"Only an idiot sticks his head in a bear trap," Fargo said. The click the hammer made as he thumbed it back was clear as could be. "One more step and I shoot your leg out from under you."

"It wouldn't stop me."

"Take that step and we'll find out." Fargo was watching the other farmers, and when one began to slip a hand under his shirt, he spun. "Keep that hand where I can see it, mister." So they were armed, after all.

The men looked at Calvin. Calvin glared at Fargo, then made as if to rush him. A gust of wind stirred the straw underfoot as the barn door was opened wider, and in strode the lord of Paradise Valley.

"What is the meaning of this?" Frank Haxton demanded. "I thought I made it plain that our guest was not to be bothered. That he has until tomorrow noon to leave of his own free will."

Calvin's arms fell to his side and he said, much like a little boy who had been caught with his hand in a cookie jar, "I found him in here with my wife. I'm only doing what any husband would do."

"I gave my word," Frank Haxton said. He gestured at the man holding Danette and the man let her go. "You disappoint me. All of you. Go get some fresh air and clear your heads. In fifteen minutes we will hold our meeting."

All the farmers save Peters filed from the barn with their heads bent in shame. Danette hesitated, then ran out.

"You too, Cal."

"I would never go against your wishes, Frank. This was personal. He had it coming."

"Perhaps he did. But I gave him my word, remember? Leave. We will talk about this later." Frank Haxton stepped aside and his lumbering follower trudged past. Haxton stared after him, saying to Fargo, "You are lucky I happened by when I did. Calvin does not know his own strength. I wish I had a hundred like him."

"Your own little army," Fargo said.

Haxton sighed. "We will never see eye to eye, will we? But I would like you to see something else." He took the lantern down, then crooked a finger. "Come along. You might find it interesting."

Most everyone was gathering by the porch. Frank Haxton walked to the west, to a spot thirty feet from the farmhouse. He handed the lantern to Fargo, sank to his knees, and began prying at the sod.

To Fargo's considerable surprise, it peeled back like thick carpet, revealing a wide door set into the earth. "A root cellar?" Normally, root cellars were under a house, not out in the yard. They were used to store food, and keep cider and the like cool in the hottest summer months.

"More or less," Haxton answered. He worked a bolt and pulled the door open. Narrow steps appeared out of pitch blackness. Bending, he ducked under a beam and descended.

Wary of a trick, Fargo followed. Before his marveling gaze unfolded an underground chamber many times the size of an ordinary root cellar. Shelves lined the walls, shelves that overflowed with food: potatoes, carrots, turnips, a haunch of jerked beef, strips of dried and jerked venison, a side of ham, a butter churn brimming with butter, molasses, cheese, coffee, tea, crackers, the list went on and on. Including a dozen tubs of water. Enough to keep a lot of people alive for a lot of months.

"Impressed? Every one of our farms has one of these. I insisted they be built before our homes were. I call them our retreats, in case of an emergency." Haxton stepped to the wall and indicated a round opening about the size of an apple. "Secret airholes keep us from suffocating."

"You think these will save you from the Apaches?"

"Why not? Even if they find us, the doors bar from within, and are reinforced to withstand the worst they can do. Plus there are gun slits so we can drive them off if need be."

Fargo had come across some lunatic propositions in his travels, but this one might be the most loco of all. "If they have to, the Apaches will wait you out. Sooner or later, you'll run out of food and water and have to go back up."

"A slim possibility, I admit," Haxton conceded. He pointed at half a dozen rifles stacked in a corner. "But if we must fight our way out, I am prepared."

"Are you prepared if they set the doors on fire and smoke you out?"

"We have plenty of water and the airholes will help against the smoke."

"Did you show these retreats of yours to Major Marshall?" Fargo asked.

"I told him about them. And do you know what he did? He told me I was the biggest damn fool he ever met, and that took some doing. His exact words! I knew right then and there that nothing I did would change his opinion."

Fargo moved to a bench covered with tools and fingered a saw. "None of this will help you. You know that, don't you?"

Haxton frowned. "I had hoped to change your mind about us, but you are the same as the major. If our forefathers had been like you, America would still be a British colony."

Fargo did not see what the two had in common. "Give up while you can. Before a lot of people die."

"Give up a dream? *My* dream?" Frank Haxton shook his head. "I would rather chop off an arm or a leg. And before you say anything, need I remind you that the people you are so worried about came here of their own free will? I did not twist anyone's arm."

"That still doesn't make it right."

"It's your opinion, not ours." Haxton walked to the steps and up out of the retreat. He had a hand on the door, ready to close it, when Fargo emerged. "I have wasted all the time I can spare on you. Remember, be gone by noon tomorrow or I will not be responsible for what my followers do to you."

"Will you let me talk to your people before I go?"

"No."

"Why not? What are you afraid of?"

"Certainly not you," Frank Haxton said. He lowered the door and slid the bolt. The sod only took a minute to replace. As Haxton unfurled he glanced to the south and his brow creased. "That's odd."

"What is?" Fargo saw only tilled fields and other farmhouses, and far to the south, the darkling needle of the south tower.

"Our sentries are supposed to keep a lantern burning all night."

"So the Apaches know where they are?"

"Scoff all you like. The lanterns are used to signal. But the sentries are safe enough. The ladders are drawn up at night as a safeguard against the towers being scaled." Haxton swelled like a barnyard rooster. "I told you before, I think of everything."

"I've seen Apaches climb sheer cliffs," Fargo mentioned. "Your towers would be child's play."

"I sincerely doubt it. Still—" Haxton cupped a hand to his mouth and bawled Calvin's name.

In thirty seconds Peters was at Frank Haxton's elbow, standing at attention as if he were a soldier. Fargo suspected Peters had been close by, eavesdropping. "Is he causing trouble?" Calvin asked.

Haxton pointed to the south. "Take two men and find out why James has let his lantern go out. Report back to me immediately."

"Yes, sir."

A premonition prompted Fargo to say, "I'd like to go along." His hunches were not always right, but it did not pay to disregard them.

"Suit yourself. Calvin, you are not to lay a finger on him. Do you understand?" Haxton commanded.

"As you wish." But to say Peters was displeased was an understatement.

Two other farmers rode with them. Fargo hung back. Not that he thought Peters would defy Haxton. But he would rather have them in front of him where he could keep an eye on them.

The sounds of the get-together at the Haxton farm faded with distance, and the night became deceptively still and peaceful. A vagrant wind stirred dust devils in a plowed field. A cow lowed in a pasture.

Fargo noticed that the first farmhouse they passed had a light in the window. The same with the second farmhouse, and so on. He asked why, when everyone was supposed to be at Haxton's.

"It's a trick," Calvin answered over his shoulder. "Frank says we're to always leave lamps on at night, even when we are not at home, so the savages will think someone is up and about."

Fargo sighed. All the Apaches had to do to learn the truth was peek in a window. Once again, Haxton was treating them as idiots.

Calvin was still talking. "Despite what Frank said, we're not done, you and me. We have unfinished business."

"And here I thought all he had to do was snap his fingers and you would lick his boots clean," Fargo said.

"You're a bastard, do you know that? But don't worry. It won't be now. Tomorrow is soon enough."

More lit farmhouses receded in their wake. They were following a broad dirt trail pockmarked by tracks. The tower was an inky silhouette against the sky, growing larger as the distance narrowed.

Fargo slid his hand to his Colt. Apaches rarely attacked at night, but it was not unheard of. Another fenced pasture materialized on their left. The cows were standing and staring toward the tower, which was peculiar. At that time of night they should be resting.

About fifty yards from the needle, Calvin Peters

slowed his buttermilk to a walk and pulled a Henry from his saddle scabbard. The other two were quick to imitate him.

Fargo kept his hand on the Colt. At night it was just as effective. He rose in the stirrups but could not pierce the murk at the tower's base. When the farmers drew rein, so did he. His saddle creaked as he dismounted.

"We'll go on foot from here," Calvin Peters said.

"What about our horses?" Fargo asked.

"What about them?"

Fargo would have thought it was obvious. "Apaches are fond of stealing them, and I'm fond of mine."

"Oh." Calvin bobbed his chin at the other two farmers. "Both of you stay with the animals. Give a holler if you hear or see anything."

"You can count on us," one said.

Calvin assumed the lead. He tried to move quietly, but his lightest tread was like the ponderous movements of a bull buffalo to Fargo's seasoned ears. Fargo stayed a few feet back, as much out of distrust as because of the possibility of an ambush by Mimbres.

Up close, the tower appeared higher than it was. It was as still as a tomb.

"James should have seen us by now," Calvin whispered. "He should have said something."

Of more interest to Fargo was the ladder. It had not been drawn up as it was supposed to be. "You keep watch and I'll go up."

"Frank put me in charge," Calvin said. "You're to do as I say, not the other way around."

"Then I'll go up and you keep watch." Fargo grinned to himself and started up the ladder before Peters could object. He was ten feet up when Calvin snarled, "Hey!" and the ladder quivered to his additional weight.

At forty feet, the wind whipped at Fargo's buckskins. Or maybe it just felt that way. Fargo had been climbing rapidly, but now he slowed, his gaze riveted on the square opening to the platform. If Apaches were waiting, they would strike the instant he poked his head up. A hand bumped his left boot and his spur jingled.

"Why have you stopped?" Calvin demanded.

Fargo regretted not letting Peters go first. "I don't want my throat slit."

"James?" Calvin softly called. "Where are you? Why has the lantern gone out? Are you up there?"

The silence was enough of an answer for Fargo, but not for the big farmer.

"Answer me, damn it! Frank sent us to check on you. You better have a good excuse."

Fargo climbed another two rungs, until his head was directly under the platform. Taking off his hat, he suddenly thrust it through the opening. Nothing happened. He jammed it back on his head and cautiously dared a look. Again, nothing happened. No war whoops, no flash of cold steel, no flare of a shot. The platform appeared to be deserted but he could only see half of it. Ascending the rest of the way, he crouched and inched to where he could verify no one else was there. "No one is here," he said.

"That can't be!" Calvin was so big he had to squeeze through the opening by pushing against the platform. "I hate coming up here," he muttered. He wrenched on his arm, and in doing so, he slammed his rifle's stock against the tower. The resulting *thump* would alert every Apache for hundreds of feet around.

Fargo braced for he knew not what, only to be taunted by more silence. Yet James *was* missing and it was doubtful he had wandered off. A thought struck him and he scanned the platform a second time. "The lantern isn't here."

"What?" Calvin turned, and swore. "Neither is the bugle. But James would never leave until someone came to relieve him." He scratched his head. "I don't get it. If the Apaches killed him, where's his body? Or did they take him alive?"

"Send one of the others up here and the rest of us will have a look around," Fargo proposed.

"All right. You wait here and keep your eyes peeled, or you might disappear too. Not that I would miss you, but Frank might blame me." Calvin chuckled and squeezed down through the opening.

Fargo made a circuit of the platform, gazing hard into the night. If the valley were any more peaceful, he would think he was in Kansas. But the Mimbres had to be to blame. It was the only explanation. Ojo Blanco was up to something. But *what*? He had a dozen burning questions, but the only ones with the answers were the Mimbres, and by the time he figured it out, it might be too late.

11

The search proved fruitless. Fargo and Calvin Peters crisscrossed the area without finding a trace of the missing sentry. Again and again Fargo dismounted and sought evidence of fresh tracks. Again and again he climbed back in the saddle disappointed.

Finally Peters instructed one of the farmers to stay at the tower until someone was sent to replace him. "For God's sake, pull up the ladder and don't let it down unless you are sure it's one of us."

The ride back to the Haxton farm was as uneventful as the ride out. They saw no one. The farmhouses stood undisturbed. Serenity reigned in Paradise Valley.

Yet Fargo was uneasy. Extremely uneasy. The missing man was not the reason. He was sure the Mimbres were responsible. No, Fargo's unease stemmed from something else, and it was all the more disquieting because he could not say exactly why he was so on edge. It was a feeling he had deep inside, a feeling spawned by he knew not what, other than a sense of foreboding. Something was gravely wrong and some part of him realized it. But try as he might to assign his unease a cause, he couldn't.

He experienced a glimmer of insight for a few fleeting seconds as they were passing yet another farmhouse with a pair of lit windows staring into the dark like glowing eyes. He glimpsed, or thought he glimpsed, a furtive form near the house. Instantly he reined the Ovaro toward it and used his spurs.

His Colt in hand, Fargo galloped to the side of the

house and came to a stop, glancing this way and that for the skulker. An empty yard laughed at him. No one was there. Nothing was disturbed. Climbing down, he checked the windows and the doors. They were latched and locked. He paced the yard to the edge of a cornfield. He stood and listened for a while. The wind laughed at him too. But had it been his imagination? The cows in a nearby pasture were all up and staring at the house. They, too, were uneasy.

Reluctantly, Fargo stepped into the stirrups. The nape of his neck felt as if it were crawling with ants. Frustrated with himself, he headed north.

Calvin and the other farmer had stopped a quarter of a mile away and were waiting for him.

"Where the hell did you get to?" Peters demanded.

"I thought I saw something."

"Next time, give a holler. I figured maybe you ran off and was about to go let Frank know."

The meeting at the Haxton farm was breaking up. Farmers and their families were heading home. Several men were on the porch with Haxton, who listened to Peters's account, then sent the oldest son of one of the farmers, a strapping youth of twenty or so, to the south tower with a lantern and orders to raise an alarm if he so much as heard a twig snap.

Fargo led the Ovaro around to the barn. He stripped off the saddle blanket, saddle, and bridle, and placed the Ovaro in an empty stall. Then he helped himself to a bucket of oats. "You've earned it," he said, and gave the pinto a pat.

A slight sound caused Fargo to spin and drop into a crouch. A figure was framed in the doorway. An hourglass figure whose hair shone in the starlight, her dress sculpted to her lush body like a second skin.

"There you are!" Tricia declared. "I've been looking all over for you. I wondered where you got to."

"Didn't your father tell you?" Fargo responded, straightening.

"He and I aren't on speaking terms at the moment. I'm mad at him." Tricia came into the barn.

121

"Over what?"

"Over you, silly," Tricia said. "I resent how he is treating you after all you have done for me." Her voice fell to a husky whisper. "And the intimate interludes we have shared."

"Does he know about those?" Fargo asked.

"Do you really think I would tell him? He would have you flayed alive, and Lord knows what he would do to me." Tricia stopped in front of him. "No, it's our little secret, now and forever."

Fargo stepped to the ladder to the hayloft and placed his foot on the bottom rung. "I'm turning in."

"Up there? I won't hear of it. You can use the sofa. It's much more comfortable than the hay would be."

"I like it better out here."

Tricia came to his side and placed a hand on his arm. "What's the matter? Don't you want to be near me?"

"I don't want to be near your father." And if Apaches were sneaking about, Fargo might catch them at it.

"But I was hoping—" Tricia stopped and glanced at the loft. A slow smile spread across her face. "Perhaps you're right. Perhaps it would be better up there than in the house."

Fargo stared at her. She couldn't mean what he thought she meant. "Better how?"

"How do you think?" Tricia pressed herself against him, her fingers rising to his neck, her lips finding his in a brief, hungry kiss.

"Are you sure it's safe?" Fargo imagined her father storming in with a rifle blazing.

"They'll be turning in soon. I told them I was going to my room and walked off in a sulk, so I don't think they'll bother to check on me." Tricia rubbed herself against him, tantalizing him with her charms. "Even if they do, they won't know where to find us."

Fargo was tempted, but he had no hankering to be the guest of honor at a strangulation jig. "Your mother and father weren't born yesterday."

Tricia had an answer for every objection. "We'll hear

122

them and I can sneak back inside." She nodded upward and grinned. "What do you say?"

"Ladies first." Fargo patted her fanny as she started to climb and she giggled. He watched her backside sway up the ladder, and went up himself. He did not close the barn door.

The loft smelled of must and dust and the hay. A pile was to one side, the rest a flat bed. Tricia sank onto her back, a hand behind her head, her body posed seductively, her right leg moving slowly back and forth. "See anything you like, handsome?"

"The hay. I can use some sleep."

Chuckling, Tricia smacked his foot and motioned for him to lie beside her. "That did wonders for my esteem."

"Women," Fargo said. He stretched out with his elbow bent and his head in his hand. "When you want it, you want it."

"Must you be so crass? We have something special. Don't spoil it." Tricia leaned toward him, her lips twin cherries. "Besides, you'll have to admit I can offer you certain treats the hay can't."

"Like what?"

"You can be so mean," Tricia grinned, and kissed him. Her mouth was molten liquid, her tongue a velvet probe. When they pulled apart she was breathing heavily and her eyelids were hooded. "That was nice. Very nice. Better than the hay can do, I daresay."

"I'm still not convinced. Prove it."

"I should chuck you out the hayloft door." Tricia molded herself to him anew, and let her lips and her fingers demonstrate. Passionate need infused her kisses and her touch. She explored every square inch of Fargo's buckskins, caressing what was under them, from his neck to his knees and back again. Her hands lingered below his waist, stroking his pole so that he bulged fit to burst from his pants.

Pausing, Tricia glanced down. "See?" she said teasingly. "I would like to see hay do that."

"Hay can't do this, either," Fargo said, and cupped

her left breast. At the contact she gasped and her lips parted in a delectable oval.

"Do you have any notion of what you do to me?"

Fargo was about to reply that he did have some notion, yes, when light suddenly filled the barn entrance. Placing a hand over Tricia's mouth, he raised a finger to his own, then swiveled so he could see over the edge. Tricia did the same, careful not to raise her head above the loft.

Calvin Peters stood just inside the barn, holding a lantern aloft. Over his shoulder he called out, "Here's his horse."

Seconds later, Frank Haxton stepped into the doorway. He walked halfway to the stall, then stopped and tapped a finger against his chin. "He's around here somewhere, then."

"Want me and some of the others to search for him?" Calvin asked.

"There's no need. He hasn't left the valley." Haxton's features darkened. "He's probably off with that willful daughter of mine. May she burn in perdition for her sinful ways."

Fargo felt Tricia stiffen.

"Should you talk like that about the fruit of your own loins?" Calvin asked her father.

"We can't deny the evidence of our own eyes," Frank Haxton said. "My daughter has a wanton nature. She chased after that good-for-nothing back in Ohio, and now she is flaunting herself over this Fargo."

"It must be hard on you and your wife."

"You have no idea," Haxton said. "As a child Tricia was always willful. She would not pay attention during Bible studies, and was forever fidgeting. She is a bad seed planted in good soil, but she refused to take root. The devil has her in his hold and the torments of hell will be her reward. If I let them be."

"What do you have in mind?"

"Her mother and I have discussed it, and Tricia is not leaving here. Ever. Young Merrill has expressed an interest. God knows why. But he will make a fine husband, and she will marry him whether she wants to or not."

"How about Fargo? I wish you would let me deal with him."

"Be patient. Soon your wish will come true," Haxton said. "We can't do anything, though, until noon tomorrow. The others might become suspicious."

"But what if Fargo doesn't leave like you told him to?"

"He will. He will want to go to Fort Craig and tell Major Marshall he has failed. You and some others will lie in wait for him. Make it look like Apaches were to blame. The heathens make dandy scapegoats."

"What about James? His parents are beside themselves. He was only sixteen."

The pair drifted out, talking in low tones, and the lantern light faded.

Fargo sat up and shifted toward Tricia. He expected her to be upset, so upset she would shed tears. But as she slowly rose on her elbows, her face and her tone mirrored a hardness that had not been there before.

"Did you hear him? My own father called me a wanton! He despises me. Me! His own daughter."

"Keep your voice down," Fargo advised.

"Now he intends to marry me off! Him and mother, both. My father wants to control my life like he does the lives of everyone else in Paradise Valley." Tricia was shaking with fury. "I won't let him. I will never marry Merrill. Do you hear me? Never!"

Fargo glanced at the barn door. No one appeared. Evidently her outburst had not been overheard.

Tricia was not done ranting. "Why did I come here? What was I thinking? That they would forgive me and all would be well? I forgot. For all my father's Bible-thumping, he practices precious little of what the Bible says. Except an eye for an eye and a tooth for a tooth."

"Maybe you should go inside," Fargo suggested. She would not want to do the other, the mood she was in.

"Why? Because I'm mad? So what? In fact, my father

has given me all the more reason not to go in. If he believes I'm a wanton, then shouldn't I act like one? It would serve him right if I stayed out all night."

"He might come looking for you if you stay out too late," Fargo mentioned.

"Good. Let him. I'd like him to find us together," Tricia said bitterly. "Think of the look on his face if he sees me in your arms."

Instead, Fargo thought of the gun that would be in Haxton's hands. "Take a few deep breaths and calm down."

"I don't want to be calm. I want you, and I want you now."

Fargo had been with all kinds of women. Timid women. Bold women. Women who were so shy they would not look at a naked man. Women who were so brazen they would rip a man's clothes off and ravish him. But few women ever ravished him as forcefully and energetically as Tricia Haxton now did. She pushed him onto his back and began tearing at his shirt and pants in a wild frenzy of desire. All he had to do was lie there and enjoy himself.

Tricia kissed his face, his ears, his neck. She nibbled at his skin with tiny, feathery bites. She traced a damp path with her tongue from his throat to his waist, then swirled the tip of her tongue around and around in his navel. Her hands were equally busy, roving high, delving low, caressing, kneading, stroking.

Fargo did his part. He sucked on her tongue and on her earlobes. He tweaked her nipples until they were flinty points of lust. He ran his palms up and down the length of her smooth thighs. But when he started to slide his hand between her legs to her womanly core, she unexpectedly pushed his forearm aside, straddled him, and deftly impaled herself on his manhood. She was a beautiful sight—her eyes hooded with carnal craving, her swollen breasts heaving with ardor, her exquisite legs splayed across his hips.

Then came the pinnacle. Tricia bucked like a mustang. She threw back her head and opened her mouth wide, but no sounds came out other than the heavy husk of her rapid breaths. Her release sent him over the brink.

Afterward, Tricia lay with her head on his shoulder and idly entwined her fingers in his hair. "Was that wanton enough?" she sleepily asked.

"You put the hay to shame." Fargo grinned and pecked her on her perspiring forehead.

Tricia tilted her face to him. "You will take me with you when you go, won't you?" Her eye pleaded with his. "I refuse to become another of my father's puppets."

"When I ride out, you go with me," Fargo promised. All they had to do was make it past Calvin Peters, and then past the Mimbres and across the parched mountains to Fort Craig.

"It can't be soon enough to suit me."

Soon the rhythmic rise and fall of Tricia's chest told Fargo she was asleep. Slumber eluded him. He had too much on his mind. He could not stop thinking about the south tower, and the missing youth, and the uneasy feeling he had on the ride back.

Minute dragged after minute. The barn was quiet. Outside, the night was tranquil. Weariness crawled through Fargo's veins and his eyelids grew leaden. He was on the threshold of dreamland when the Ovaro nickered. Struggling up through mental soup, he opened his eyes. He felt movement and thought Tricia was stirring, but no, she was still sound asleep. Belatedly, he realized the loft had moved ever so slightly under him.

Someone was climbing the ladder.

Fargo drew his Colt. He slid his finger through the trigger guard and around the trigger and placed his thumb on the hammer.

A head rose out of the gloom. Fargo was expecting Frank Haxton or Calvin Peters. But the head was not wearing a hat, and the head had long hair, not short. Hair as black as the night, hair contained by a wide band across the brow.

It was an Apache.

Their eyes locked. Neither moved. Fargo had Tricia on top of him and she was within easy reach of the knife the warrior held in his right hand. He figured the Mimbre must be as startled as he was, otherwise the man would have attacked the instant he saw them. For long, tense heartbeats neither of them moved. Then Tricia started as if she had been pricked with a pin and slowly sat up, saying, "My goodness. How long have I been asleep?"

Tricia was between Fargo and the Apache and blocked his view of the Apache's knife. He galvanized into motion. Hurling her to his left, he surged up off the hay. The knife was streaking at his chest. He fired from the hip, and the slug caught the Mimbre high in the forehead and sent him toppling from the ladder. Fargo sprang to the edge of the loft and saw the body hit. He took aim but a second shot was not needed.

Shock transfixed Tricia, until shouts arose from the farmhouse. "My parents!" she exclaimed, and snatched at her clothes. For all her brave talk earlier, she was still terrified of them.

"Stay up here." Fargo quickly pulled his pants up. He slid his legs over the side and hurried down. As his feet touched the ground, other feet pounded in the yard.

Once again, lantern light dispelled the darkness. Frank Haxton rushed in, wearing his nightshirt, a Henry in his other hand. "What the devil!" he blurted. "Fargo! Where have you been?"

"Sleeping in the loft."

"Have you seen my dau—" Haxton saw the body, and turned to stone. "A Mimbre? Here? What in the world is going on?"

"That's what I would like to know." Fargo scanned the barn, but the warrior appeared to have been alone. "He was climbing up into the hayloft."

Haxton walked over, holding the lantern high for a better look. "He must have heard you snoring. You were lucky you woke up when you did."

Fargo let him jump to the wrong conclusion. "Have the Mimbres ever done anything like this?"

"No. But they skulk around all the time, the lousy vermin," Haxton growled. "There still hasn't been any sign of James."

"But why the hayloft?"

"I told you. He heard you snore. Or maybe you rolled over and he heard the hay rustle. What difference does it make? You're alive and he's dead. Thank your Maker you are still alive." Haxton nudged the still form. "First thing come daylight, I'll hang this one by his heels from the cottonwood out front. It will serve as a warning to the rest of his kind."

"And make the Mimbres madder."

"As if I care." Haxton bent down. "You don't suppose this is Ojo Blanco, do you? I've never set eyes on him."

"It's not."

"Too bad. He's the one who most deserves to be lying here." Haxton spat in the Apache's face, and stepped back. "I'm grateful for what you've done. He might have tried to break into the house. But it doesn't change anything. I still want you out of my valley by noon."

"I wouldn't expect you to change your mind," Fargo said dryly.

Haxton made a "harrrrumph" sound, wheeled, and stalked off.

Bits of straw fell from the loft as Tricia swung onto the ladder and carefully descended. "I never realized until this moment just how despicable my father is." She fluffed at her hair. "If I never see him again after tomorrow, I won't shed a tear over it."

Fargo replaced the spent cartridge and moved to the door. A welcome breeze fanned his face. In the distance, a dog barked. To the north reared the sentry tower, a lantern glowing on the platform. A light was also on in the farmhouse, but all the curtains had been drawn and no one was peering out.

Tricia's arm brushed his. "I'll sneak in the front, and if they ask, I'll tell them I went for a long walk." She kissed his cheek and went to go.

"I'll tag along."

"Why?" Tricia tittered. "I'm perfectly capable of finding my way in the dark, thank you."

Fargo pointed at the body. "Where there is one there might be more."

They reached the porch without being attacked. Fargo stayed in the shadows while she crept to the door and inserted her key. She pushed but the door would not open.

"It's bolted on the inside," Tricia whispered. She did not seem concerned. Beckoning, she led him around the side to a dark window. "I left this unlatched, just in case."

Fargo thought of the Apache, and how lucky she was the Mimbre had gone to the barn instead of the house. She slipped inside, blew him a kiss, and eased the window down.

The Mimbre. Fargo stood in the barn entrance and stared at the body, and tried to shake off his unease. It was worse now. He had a feeling, a hunch, call it whatever he might, that he was overlooking something— something important, something that could spell life or death for the inhabitants of Paradise Valley.

The missing sentry. The strange behavior of the cows. The barking dogs. The Mimbre who climbed to the hayloft. They were connected. Fargo was sure. And if he could piece together exactly how they were linked, he could save a lot of women and children, and the foolish husbands and fathers who had dragged their families into the fierce heart of the Mimbres Mountains.

Ojo Blanco was the key. He hated whites, and he would not rest until Haxton and his followers were wiped out. Ojo Blanco was also crafty. Whatever plan he came up with would be cunning and almost certain of success. Ojo Blanco would leave little to chance. The plan must take into account everything Ojo Blanco knew about whites, and exploit their weakness.

The Mimbres had attacked once in force and been repulsed. The trumpets had sounded and the whites had rallied, and their Henrys turned the tide of conflict. What had Ojo Blanco learned from that clash? Were the sentries the weak link? Was that why James had been taken?

Fargo gazed from the crumpled form to the hayloft to the Haxton farmhouse. The whites were few but had many repeating rifles and bullets. The Mimbres were many but had few repeating rifles, and would be driven off again unless they could stop the whites from using their repeaters.

It hit him, then, like a splash of ice-cold water in the face. Fargo knew what Ojo Blanco was up to. The plan was brilliant, and unless Fargo acted right away, the settlers would not live out the day.

12

The nearest farm belonged to Calvin Peters. Fargo rode over alone. It would not do to wake up Haxton and have him barge about, waking up every settler and creating a commotion bound to be noticed by the Mimbres.

The farm lay undisturbed under the stars. Fargo drew rein fifty yards out, dismounted, and removed his spurs. He slid them into a saddlebag, then shucked the Henry.

Surprise was on his side, but that did not count for much. If his hunch was right, more than likely the Apache would spot him before he spotted the Apache. But he had to try.

The barn door was closed. Fargo pulled with one hand but it would not open. Setting down the Henry, he tried with both hands and was rewarded with a loud creak from the top hinge. Rigid with tension, he listened for some indication the Apache had heard, but no sounds came from within. Another pull, and the gap was wide enough for him to scoop up the Henry and slip inside.

Instantly, Fargo stepped to the right and crouched. It was as inky as a cave. All he could make out were vague objects: the stalls, the square bulk of the feed bin, the hayloft. Groping carefully, he found the ladder. Climbing was easy enough, but halfway up he stopped. The smart thing, he reflected, was to wait for daylight. But that might be when Ojo Blanco planned to attack. Girding himself, he edged higher a rung at a time.

The hay greeted his wary gaze. Fargo carefully placed one foot on the loft, and then the other. The Henry ready, he moved toward a mound. The Mimbre could be anywhere. Fargo had to flush him out without getting killed. He nearly bumped into a long, slender pole, and stopped. Gripping it in his left hand, he tucked the handle under his left arm and lifted the pitchfork.

Again and again Fargo thrust the tines into the hay. From side to side and back again, he lanced the pitchfork in as far as it would go, expecting at any moment to spear human flesh. But there was only the hay.

Baffled, Fargo dropped the pitchfork and moved to the ladder. He had been so sure, but he had been wrong. So much for outguessing Ojo Blanco. He descended and walked out. Save for a tree between the barn and the house, the yard was empty.

A voice in the house stopped Fargo in his tracks. Someone was up! Dashing to the tree, he hid behind the trunk. A couple of minutes went by and no lamps were lit. No one appeared at the rear door. Figuring it was safe, he turned to go back to the Ovaro.

Fargo could not say what made him look up. He had not heard anything. He had not sensed anything. He just happened to glance into the branches overhead and noticed that one of the limbs was twice as thick as all the rest. Thicker, and a lighter shade, or part of it was. The upper half. A trick of the shadows, Fargo reckoned, until a gust of wind fluttered the leaves and something that was not leaves, something long and fine that hung over both sides of the branch. Something that could only be human hair.

The Mimbre launched himself from the limb like a mountain lion springing from ambush. Fargo brought the Henry up, but a bronzed shoulder slammed into him before he could fire and cold steel sought his heart. He had to let go of the rifle to clutch the warrior's knife arm, even as the impact bore him to earth.

The Mimbre grunted and locked the thick fingers of his other hand on Fargo's throat. Fargo wrapped a hand around the other's wrist, but he could not push the hand off, and within seconds his lungs were straining for the air that was being denied.

The tip of the knife dipped lower. Another three or four inches and it would sink into Fargo's chest. He bucked upward, but the Apache was too heavy. He tried to roll to the right, but the Mimbre's knees held him in place.

Fargo's throat was on fire. His shoulder throbbed with the effort of holding the knife at bay. Unable to breathe, he was rapidly weakening. He must do something and he must do it quickly.

Suddenly shifting, Fargo relaxed his hold on the Apache's knife arm. It had the desired effect; the knife swept past his neck to embed itself in the dirt. It also brought the Mimbre's face close to his own. He smashed his forehead against the warrior's nose and heard the *crunch* of cartilage. The Mimbre instinctively drew back. Once more Fargo smashed his forehead into him, into the Mimbre's mouth, pulping the warrior's lips. The warrior would not release his hold, though.

In desperation, Fargo crooked his right knee and groped wildly at his boot. The hilt of the Arkansas toothpick molded to his palm. He drew it without the warrior being aware.

The world about him was fading to black when Fargo plunged the doubled-edge blade into the Mimbre's side four times, clear to the hilt. At each stab the warrior shuddered, and on the last, he exhaled loudly and collapsed.

Fargo pushed, but he lacked the strength to shove the body off. Taking deep breaths, he stared up through the branches at the stars. His hunch had been right, after all. But it was obvious he could not do it alone. He needed help. Like it or not, he must ask the farmers.

A damp sensation was spreading across his buckskin shirt. The Mimbre's blood, Fargo realized. Again he pushed, and this time succeeded. Slowly rising, he rubbed his throat and walked to the farmhouse. He pounded on the door until an angry shout resulted.

"Who is it? What do you want?"

Fargo identified himself, and stepped back as the door

was wrenched open and the muzzle of a rifle was shoved in his face.

"What is this? What the hell are you doing here this late?" Calvin Peters demanded. "You better have a good excuse, mister."

"Is that good enough?" Fargo pointed at the dead Mimbre.

Calvin raised his lamp and, as its glow spread, swore lustily. "What's going on? Where did that redskin come from?"

"There is a Mimbre at each farm," Fargo explained, "waiting for a signal tomorrow from Ojo Blanco." He went on to explain how the Mimbres had slipped into the valley after slaying the sentry at the south tower.

"Those devils!" Calvin exclaimed. "When the alarm is given, they'll jump us and keep us busy while the rest pour into the valley! Is that their scheme?"

"Something like that. But it won't work if we root out those already here before daybreak."

Calvin regarded him thoughtfully. "You just saved my life. And everyone else's. We're in your debt, mister."

"Don't count your chickens just yet," Fargo cautioned. "There are fifteen more farms to check. I'll ride on to the next while you go get Haxton." He did not wait for an answer but wheeled and jogged to the pinto.

Fargo did not know who the next farm belonged to. Like the rest, it was quiet and dark save for one lit window. He dismounted well out of earshot, let the Ovaro's reins dangle, and stalked forward through a cornfield. The corn grew to within a stone's throw of the house. A few feet shy of the end, he stopped and crouched. One Apache had been in a barn, the other in a tree. Where would this one be? He was about to slink toward them when movement registered.

The small hayloft door was open, framing a face fixed on the house. Fargo had a clear shot, but the blast would carry the length of the valley and make the other Apaches more vigilant.

Fargo ducked down. The Mimbre had not seen him.

Sidling to his left between the corn stalks, he circled wide until he was out of sight. Then, rising, he cat-footed to the side of the barn and on to the front corner. His back flush to the boards he sidestepped along the front wall. The hayloft door was now directly above him, the rope to the winch swaying slightly in the breeze.

Fargo pulled on the main door. If the hinges creaked, the Apache would be forewarned, but to Fargo's relief they didn't, and in a few moments he had slipped inside. Silently he crept to where he could see the loft and the squat figure outlined in the loft door. He raised the Henry and waited.

The Mimbre might as well be sculpted from stone. But that was typical. Apaches could stay perfectly still for hours, an ability ingrained at an early age. They were masterful hunters and supremely efficient killers, whether their prey was game or men.

Fargo thought of Ojo Blanco, and how the Mimbre leader must relish the prospect of wiping out the whites in the valley. Sneaking warriors in was a brilliant tactic, yet another in a long list of examples of why Apaches had been able to resist the Spanish and Mexican governments for so long, and were now successfully keeping the might of the United States Army at bay.

Fargo would never admit as much in a saloon full of bigoted drunks, but he held a grudging respect for any tribe that fought for its territory. To him it was not a matter of race. He was not one of those whites who hated anyone and everyone whose skin was different.

As much as Fargo might admire them, though, he could not condone the massacre of innocents. He would not let women and children be slaughtered.

It was a shame. Once, before Americans began streaming west of the Mississippi River like giant swarms of locusts, most whites and Indians had gotten along. The early trappers and mountain men had taken Indian wives and lived as the Indians did. Some whites still sought to live in harmony, but the majority were for exterminating the red man, or forcing them to uproot and live on land the whites did not want. The result was bloodshed and more bloodshed, with no end in sight.

Sounds intruded on Fargo's reverie. Hooves drummed in the night. Frank Haxton and Calvin Peters, coming to find him.

The statue by the loft door finally moved. The Mimbre leaned out, then jerked back and turned, no doubt to conceal himself in case the new arrivals came into the barn. Suddenly, the warrior froze.

Fargo could not see the Apache's face, but he swore he could feel hostile eyes sear into him. He had not done anything to give his presence away, but Apaches were noted for their keen eyesight.

The Mimbre had spotted him.

A screech rent the barn and the warrior came flying over the edge of the loft, a knife held high for a fatal stroke. Fargo fired when the man was in midair, the boom of the Henry unnaturally loud.

The impact flipped the Apache so that he crashed to the ground on his side. He heaved onto a knee, flailed a few times at empty air, then pitched onto his face and was still.

Fargo cautiously went closer. Often, mortally wounded Apaches were known to play dead to lure their slayers in close. But this one wasn't faking. The slug had cored his sternum and gone straight through his heart.

There were voices. The barn door opened and in marched Frank Haxton. He stared at the dead Mimbre, then did as he had done to the Mimbre at his farm; he spat on it.

"Lord, how I hate these red scum. This makes three, from what Calvin has told me. Well done. You have my thanks."

"I didn't do it for you."

"I didn't think you did," Haxton responded with a smirk. "But every Apache you kill does me another favor." He paused. "Now then, as I understand it, time is crucial. We must visit each farm and dispose of each redskin, and we must do it before sunrise. Is that right?"

"That's a start. Then you should round all your people up and leave before Ojo Blanco attacks."

"You never give up, do you? Leave our new homes and all our belongings?" Haxton laughed. "I thought I had made myself clear. This valley is ours, and will stay ours for as long as we draw breath."

"The Mimbres will never stop trying to drive you out."

"Let them. We have bested them at every turn and shall continue to do so. Eventually they will get it through their thick heads that there is no beating us."

"Apaches never give up either," Fargo persisted.

"Oh, please. You make it sound like they are invincible. The dead redskin at your feet proves otherwise." Haxton took several steps toward the yard, then stopped and looked back. "Are you coming? Or do you want us to take care of the rest by ourselves?"

Fargo had half a mind to let them. But there were the families to think of. It always came back to the women and children. "I'll lend a hand."

"Don't put yourself out on our account," was Frank Haxton's retort. To Calvin Peters he said, "Go wake up Horace. How he slept through all this noise, I'll never know. Tell him to be dressed and ready to ride in five minutes. We'll go to the Vrain farm next, and from there work our way down the valley."

The Ovaro was where Fargo had left it. He reached the barn just as the farmer called Horace emerged from the farmhouse, tucking his shirt in. Little was said. In a grim group they trotted to the next farm. Fargo let the farmers handle it. Haxton had them separate and approach from different points of the compass.

The Mimbre at this farm, like the second one Fargo had found, was in a tree near the house. Like the others, the warrior had a knife, not a rifle. Probably so they could kill silently and get their hands on a Henry without giving themselves away.

Haxton did not ask the Mimbre to come down. He did not demand the warrior surrender. He and the other farmers opened fire simultaneously, and the Mimbre smashed to earth a riddled ruin.

138

Then it was on to another farm, and the one after that. At each, an Apache was slain. At each, another farmer was added to the ranks of the seekers.

At the tenth farm, they could not find a Mimbre. They searched the barn. They scoured the trees. They trampled a flower garden and poked into every possible hiding place.

It was Fargo, who had hung back, who glimpsed a furtive form on the farmhouse roof. He shouted a warning as the Apache leaped. Four guns roared, and like a game bird crippled in midflight, the warrior tumbled.

At the next farm, no Mimbre was to be found. They hunted low and high but came across no trace of one. "He heard the shots and skedaddled like the yellow cur he is," was Haxton's opinion.

"One of these days the Mimbres will show you just how wrong you are," Fargo mentioned.

"I'd like to have them try," Frank Haxton blustered.

Suddenly, one of the other farmers pointed and exclaimed, "Look there! Isn't that the varmint?"

A darkling figure was racing swiftly westward on foot. At a yell from Calvin Peters, the farmers spurred their mounts in pursuit. The Mimbre was fleet, but the horses soon rode him down. A rifle cracked, and another, but to hit a target from horseback was hard enough; from a moving horse at night it was virtually impossible.

The Mimbre disappeared into a wheat field.

"Spread out!" Haxton bellowed. "Form a circle!"

"But we'll trample some of the wheat!" someone objected.

"One less Apache is worth a few less bushels," Haxton replied. "Move! All of you! Or he'll slip from our grasp!"

They plunged in and formed a large circle, and slowly tightened the ring, but the Mimbre eluded them. Haxton did not waste any more time. He raced to the next farm. It was the same there; the Mimbre was gone. On to the next, and by then it was apparent that the rest of the infiltrators had made for the mountains.

At the last farmhouse a grisly discovery was made.

Fargo was at the back of the pack when oaths and

cries of horror burst from the farmers. Bodies littered the yard, the bodies of the man who lived there and his whole family. As near as Fargo could reconstruct the slaughter by torchlight, the farmer had heard the ruckus from up the valley and ventured outside with his wife and children. The retreating Apaches had jumped them. Judging by the trampled grass, the farmer and his oldest son put up a terrific fight but were ultimately overwhelmed. None of the family had been mutilated, a clue that the Mimbres were in a hurry. Two small children, twins about eight years old, had their throats slit. Another girl of fourteen or so had been stabbed in the chest. The mother's body lay across hers, shielding it with her own. A knife wound between the mother's shoulder blades glistened damply. The oldest son had five knife wounds. The farmer had the rear of his head bashed in.

Frank Haxton ordered that the bodies be laid out in a row. Then he paced back and forth, ranting about the vile nature of the red race and the retribution he would bring down on the heads of the Mimbres.

"Need we any further proof that we are dealing with animals? Look at sweet little Trish and Tracy, so hideous in death! Look at Mrs. Tanner, who gave her own life to vainly try and save Mary. And Able, who must have fought like Samson fought the Philistines!"

Fargo took hold of the Ovaro's reins and walked on past the barn. He had no desire to hear the rest of Haxton's raving. The time would be better spent preparing for Ojo Blanco's attack. For as surely as he stood there, the Mimbres would soon strike, with all the warriors they could muster.

He tried to put himself in Ojo Blanco's moccasins. If the Mimbres were at full strength, they could send a hundred warriors in from several directions at once. But they would not rush headlong into the repeating rifles of the waiting settlers. Ojo Blanco would want to reduce the risk to the Mimbres as much as possible. The ideal way was to sneak in close, where the Henrys could not be used to full effect, and where the advantage of Mimbre numbers would decide the battle in the Mimbres' favor.

Fargo mulled it over long and hard, then ambled back to the yard. Frank Haxton was still pacing and speaking.

"We will bury our poor friends. Each of us will return to our homes and arm our families. At first light we will retire to our special shelters and wait out the day. If the heathens do not attack, the day after we will resume work as usual."

"No," Fargo said.

Haxton sniffed as if he had been assailed by an offensive odor. "I beg your pardon? You have no say in what we do."

"The lives of sixteen families are at stake," Fargo noted. "Outsider or not, you should hear me out."

Support came from an unlikely source. "What harm can it do, Frank?" Calvin Peters asked.

"Very well," Haxton said stiffly. "Just so everyone remembers that I have the final say."

Fargo gave them his honest opinion. "You stand a better chance if you stand together. Cut off in your cellars, the Mimbres can burn you out or wait until you run out of food and water—"

Frank Haxton was quick to interrupt. "As I have already shown you, we have enough of both in each cellar to last weeks."

"Weeks aren't forever," Fargo countered. "The Mimbres will have your cattle to eat, and all the water they need from the stream. They can outlast you. You'll be forced out into the open and killed before you can get off a shot. Or taken captive and have worse done to you and your loved ones."

"He has a point," said a farmer called Broder.

"The Lord won't let that happen to us," Frank Haxton declared.

"Still," said another farmer, named Trimble, "I would rather fight outside than be cooped up in a hole in the ground."

Haxton sighed and put his hands on his hips. "Haven't we been all through this time and again? Trust me. Trust my judgment."

Fargo gestured at the row of bodies. "This family

trusted you. Look at where it got them." Shaking his head, he faced the others. "The only hope you have is if you stand together. Even then, there are less than sixty of you left, counting your wives and children, against three hundred Apaches."

"How many?" Trimble asked in alarm.

Fargo repeated the figure. "It's how many the army estimates the Mimbres can muster."

The farmers began talking among one another in low voices.

Frank Haxton took a step and raised an arm for attention. "Of course he claims there are that many! He wants you to take his advice, not mine."

"Can you afford to ignore my advice if I'm right?" Fargo argued.

Haxton scowled. "The military always inflates the number of their enemies to justify the money our government spends on troops and forts. But I would stake my life on the fact there aren't more than a hundred Mimbre bucks, if that."

"You're not just staking your life," Fargo said. "You're staking the life of everyone here. Each man should have the right to make up his own mind."

Calvin Peters cleared his throat. "I agree."

Silence fell. Frank Haxton glared at his hulking subordinate, the corner of his mouth twitching with suppressed anger. "Do my ears deceive me? Are you siding with him?"

"I would never go against you, Frank, you know that," Calvin said. "But we have our wives and kids to think of. And I don't much like the notion of being cooped up underground, either. I never have."

Another farmer nodded vigorously. "We should gather everyone together, like he suggests, and hole up in one of the farmhouses."

Some of the men nodded. Others spoke up, agreeing with Calvin.

Frank Haxton clenched his fists and looked fit to throw himself at Fargo, but he controlled his temper. "I can not believe this."

"Don't take it personal, Frank," Calvin said. "We just want what is best for our families."

"And I don't?" Haxton nearly shouted. "Our underground retreats will work, I tell you."

"I'm a man, not a rat," Broder said. "I'd rather fight out in the open."

Other farmers nodded.

Frank Haxton paced in a circle, muttering under his breath. Finally he spun on them and said harshly, "Very well. Never let it be said I am a tyrant. We will do as you want. But make no mistake. Our fate will be on your shoulders. On all of yours. And heaven help us if you are wrong."

Fargo had a small victory to his credit. But it was not enough. It was nowhere near enough. Unless he could get them to leave the valley, they were doomed. And he was doomed along with them.

13

It did not surprise Fargo that Frank Haxton picked his own farm as the one to make their stand. At dawn, families began heading for the north end of Paradise Valley, most in the Conestogas that had brought them from points east of the Mississippi River.

Word had spread about the Mimbres hidden at the farms, and Fargo's part in discovering them. The settlers were friendlier, but not overly so. He kept to himself, leaning against the barn while family after family arrived, listening to Frank Haxton bellow orders. The man loved to hear himself bark commands.

Calvin Peters and Danette arrived. Fargo nodded at her and lifted a hand in greeting, but she would not acknowledge he was alive. Calvin, by contrast, smiled and waved.

Shortly after, perfume wreathed him and warm fingers found his shoulder. "Good morning, handsome. Or should I call you hero?"

"My name will do."

Tricia grinned and brushed his shoulder with hers. "My father is madder than a wet cat. He does not like to be upstaged."

"He would rather be dead?" Fargo caught sight of Frank glaring at them, and smiled as sweetly as he knew how. Haxton's glare became downright withering.

"Sometimes I wonder if he thinks he *can* die," Tricia said. "He truly believes God has chosen him to lead these people, and that the Lord will not let anyone or anything stand in the way of his great vision. That includes the Apaches."

Fargo grunted. Haxton was not unique. Plenty of whites thought their faith would ward off bullets and arrows, only to learn too late that to hostiles in general, and Apaches in particular, a white man with faith was the same as a white man without—just another enemy to be slain.

"My father is hoping the Mimbres don't show," Tricia went on. "He said at breakfast that it will show everyone you don't know as much as you think you do, and that they should trust in his judgment, not yours."

"I hope they don't show too." With so many lives in the balance, Fargo would love to be proven wrong.

"But they will, won't they? Before this day is done."

Fargo nodded.

"Be truthful with me. What chance do these people have?"

Fargo looked around. The mothers and daughters and younger children had been ushered into the house. The fathers and sons over the age of fourteen were positioned at intervals around a perimeter consisting of wagons, and bales of hay and straw hastily erected as a barrier. "Not a snowball's chance in hell."

"Even with all their rifles?"

"Even if a company of soldiers were here to help," Fargo said. "Everyone here is going to die and there's not a damn thing I can do to prevent it."

"You hold the Apaches in high regard," Tricia observed.

"Only a jackass doesn't," was Fargo's rejoinder.

"Aren't you scared? I am. I don't want to stay but I can't leave my parents. As bullheaded as my father is, as wrong as he can be, he is still my father, and I still love him."

The last of the families arrived in an overloaded Conestoga. They had packed every possession of value, everything from clothes to a rocking chair that lay atop the pile. Haxton chided the man for taking so long, and the man blamed his wife for wanting to bring everything but the stove.

"People sure are strange critters," Tricia commented. "We don't do what is good for us even when not doing it will get us killed." She idly swiped at a stray lock of hair. "If the worst comes to pass, do me a favor, will you? Don't let me fall into their clutches. I couldn't stand that."

"They don't always kill women."

Tricia averted her face. "That's what I couldn't stand. I don't hate them like my father does. But I don't care to spend the rest of my days in a wickiup or whatever the Apaches call them. Will you promise or not?"

"I'll do what I can. But I might be too busy to help you," Fargo admitted. "Find a revolver. Keep one cartridge in the cylinder to use if you have to."

"That takes courage. A special kind of courage I sadly lack. As much as I want to, I couldn't," Tricia said forlornly. "I'm counting on you."

Her mother called her name.

"I have to go. They want all the women inside. We're each to take a window. But between you and me, if the Apaches get inside, it will all be over sooner than you can say lickety-split." Tricia gave him a tender squeeze, then pivoted and hurried indoors.

Nine o'clock came and went. Ten o'clock. Eleven. Shortly before noon, Frank Haxton and Calvin Peters detached themselves from a wagon and came over.

Haxton was as temperamental as ever. "Well? Where are they? Surely if the savages were going to attack they would have done so by now." He nudged Calvin. "This is what we get for listening to him. Half a day wasted."

No sooner were the words out of his mouth than from far to the south wafted the sharp notes of a bugle. They quickened to a feverish frenzy, then abruptly ended in a metallic bleat.

Scarcely able to credit his ears, Fargo whirled on Frank Haxton. "You didn't recall your sentries?"

"No. Why should I? We needed to be forewarned.

146

Evidently you were right and I was wrong. The heathens are on their way."

The bugle electrified the farmers. They scurried about, taking up posts, handing out ammunition. Trimble and Broder brought the ladder out of the barn and leaned it against the side. Presently, after much scrambling and nearly slipping off the roof twice, Trimble reached the top of the barn and hunkered, his right hand shielding his eyes from the harsh glare of the blazing sun.

"Anything?" Frank Haxton shouted up.

"Not yet," Trimble replied. "Maybe Malcolm was mistaken. Maybe he only thought he saw them and blew the bu—" Trimble's head jerked and he blurted, "Wait! What's this?"

"What's what?" Haxton impatiently demanded.

"Smoke. Rising from the south tower, unless I am mistaken. The Apaches have set it on fire."

Calvin Peters's jaw muscles twitched. "It's started, then. They'll work their way up the valley, burning as they come. Our homes and our crops. All our hard work, all the building and the planting, it all will have been in vain."

"Nothing is ever in vain," Haxton said. "We will start over. We will rebuild. We will plant new seeds. Paradise Valley will live up to its name."

"I'm not so sure, Frank."

Haxton was so shocked that his mouth moved, but no sounds came out until he sputtered, "Get thee behind me, Satan!"

Trimble was on his feet on the roof. "More smoke!" he excitedly cried. "From the Steadman farmhouse and barn!"

"They're all dead," Frank Haxton said, as if that were of any consequence.

"I can see riders!" Trimble shouted. "Groups of them, moving at the far end of the valley. Not many as yet, but they are heading our way."

"It will take them a while to destroy everything," Haxton said.

If that was supposed to give the other farmers some

small comfort, it failed miserably. They looked at one another like men teetering on the brink of a cliff.

"We made a mistake coming here," Calvin Peters remarked.

Frank Haxton spun on him. "Stop talking like that! When have I ever let you down? We *will* win the day! And I will expect you to apologize for your lack of trust."

Fargo turned on him. "It's now or never, Haxton."

"What is?"

"It's not too late. Get these people in those wagons and get them the hell out of here. Now. Right this instant."

"Be serious."

Fargo could not keep the desperation out of his voice. "They're dead if you don't. Each and every man, woman, and child. But if you start for the mountains, you can reach them before the Mimbres get there. Most of you will be saved."

"How can it be that you haven't realized by now that we are not going anywhere? You're wasting your breath."

Fargo shifted toward Peters. "Calvin? The others will listen to you. Do it. Do it now."

The big farmer looked sheepishly at Haxton, then bowed his chin. "I'm sorry. I can't."

Trimble had moved to the south end of the roof. "Apaches are in among the cows! Do you hear them? Dear God in heaven, do you hear them?"

The cows were lowing. Not as they normally would, in tranquil contentment, but loudly, fearfully, painfully. They were lowing because they were being slaughtered. They were worth a lot of money south of the border, or would feed the Mimbres for many months, but Ojo Blanco preferred to erase every trace of the hated white settlement, including the livestock.

Just then a drawn-out yelp eclipsed the lowing, a yelp made by an animal in its terror-stricken death throes.

"They're killing our dogs!" a farmer cried.

"I knew I should have brought mine with me," another said sadly.

Worry spread like a contagion. Men nervously fingered their rifles and stared to the south in mutual horror.

Trimble had both hands shielding his eyes now. "There must be six farms on fire, maybe more! I never saw so much smoke! Some of the cows are loose and are running around all confused."

The mention of the smoke troubled Fargo. He moved to where he could see it better, puzzled as to why it should prick at him like a sharp razor.

One of the farmers was being restrained by others. "Let me go!" he screeched. "They'll burn my place soon and I have to stop them!"

"Be sensible, Joe," Broder said.

"The Apaches are closer!" Trimble shouted down. "Lordy, there are so many! More than we ever reckoned! Fargo was right!"

Figures were visible from the ground, too. The Apaches were sweeping up the valley, some invading farmhouses and setting them ablaze, others going from pasture to pasture to deal with the cattle.

Pasty faces were pressed to every window in the Haxton house. The women and small children were helpless witnesses to the spreading conflagration. The frightened lowing of the cattle, the piercing howls of the dogs, the thick cloud of smoke growing thicker by the minute, the sight of red-and-orange flames leaping from the rooftops of distant and not-so-distant buildings—even the men were afraid, but trying hard not to show it.

Fargo could not take his eyes off the smoke. Something about it gnawed at him like a beaver's teeth at a tree trunk. A great gray mantle covered half the valley and was slowly spreading north. Gray tentacles writhed ahead of the mass like the questing tentacles of an aerial octopus.

"If it keeps spreading like it is," Calvin Peters commented, "that smoke will reach us before too long."

Fargo took a half step back as if he had been struck.

It hit him, then. He knew it all. He knew why Ojo Blanco had not bothered to wipe them out the other day at the ravine. He knew why Ojo Blanco had waited so long to retaliate for the earlier defeat. And he knew how Ojo Blanco intended to render the Henrys next to useless.

The wily Mimbre had been patiently waiting for just the right day.

Paradise Valley ran from north to south. Normally, the wind blew from west to east. Which meant that smoke from a fire would be borne east, away from the valley. But now and again the wind blew from different directions. It might be from north to south. Or, more rarely, from south to north. And it was exactly such a day Ojo Blanco had waited for. A day when the smoke from burning farms in the south part of the valley would be wafted north toward farms as yet untouched, until eventually the entire valley was covered with smoke from end to end, an acrid fog that made it hard to breathe and harder still to see anything more than a dozen feet away.

By a quirk of fate, Ojo Blanco was using smoke to take lives, just as the other day Fargo had used it to save Tricia's and his. "Damn," Fargo said aloud.

"What?" Frank Haxton was gazing at the figures in the distance with a haughty confidence born of ignorance. "I should shoot you, but why deprive the Apaches. You're dead anyway."

"So you keep saying."

"Ojo Blanco figured out how to make your Henry repeaters next to useless," Fargo revealed.

"He wishes they were," Haxton responded. "Once the heathens are in range, we will mow them down in droves."

"Not if you can't see them until they're right on top of you."

"And how will Ojo Blanco accomplish that miracle?" Frank Haxton sarcastically quizzed.

"The smoke will do it for him." Fargo bobbed his chin.

Haxton laughed the idea to scorn. "A little smoke won't stop our bullets. We will mow them down like a scythe through grass, I tell you."

"Dear God," Calvin Peters breathed. He had heard.

"Don't listen to him, Cal," Haxton said. "He wasn't here when we drove the savages off the last time. He has no idea what we are capable of."

Fargo sighed. "I know what Apaches are capable of. Please, Haxton. I'm begging you. Get everyone out of here before it's too late. You stand a better chance of holding the Mimbres off in the mountains. Head for Fort Craig, and in a week or two you'll be safe."

"Oh, you would like that, wouldn't you? I should have guessed. Yet another ploy of yours to have us give in to the military's demands. But it won't work. We are staying and fighting for what is ours."

"But the smoke," Calvin Peters said.

"I worry about you, Calvin. You are starting to carp more than my wife." Haxton scanned their defenses. "But if you keep your wits about you, as I have done, you will notice that the savages have made the mistake of coming at us from one direction and one direction only. Round up a third of the men on the east, west and north sides, and reinforce the south perimeter. At my command, we will show those devils that they can never get the better of us." He waited, and when Peters did not move, he testily demanded, "Well? What are you waiting for?"

"I'm sorry, but I think we should head for the mountains like Fargo wants."

"Use your brain, will you? Do you really want all our wives and children out in the open where the Apaches can pick us off at their leisure?"

After a long interval Calvin said quietly, "No, I suppose not."

"Then quit dawdling. The sands of time are wasting while you stand there like a great dumb ox."

"Don't call me dumb," Calvin said, but he did as he was bid and hastened toward a Conestoga.

Up on the barn roof Trimble cupped a hand to his mouth. "Frank! Two Apaches are coming our way under a flag of truce!"

Fargo had already spotted them. Ojo Blanco and another warrior were slowly riding toward the farm, the other warrior holding a long pole with a white towel tied to one end.

"What are they up to?" Frank Haxton asked. "They have never asked to parley before."

"I'll go with you," Fargo offered.

"Are you insane? I'm not riding out there. What if it's a trick? I'm too valuable to take the risk. It wouldn't be fair to the others."

"Is that so?"

"Without me to lead them they don't stand a prayer. It's me and me alone who has guided them, held them together, saved them from their own folly. In a crisis they look to me and, as their shepherd, I must not let them down."

Ojo Blanco and his companion had reined up just out of rifle range and were waiting for the whites to acknowledge their presence.

"They only want to talk," Fargo said.

"Are you willing to swear on the Bible to that? I don't share your confidence in heathens."

"Then I'll go myself," Fargo proposed. Jogging to the Ovaro, he shoved his Henry into the saddle scabbard, gripped the saddle horn, and swung up. All eyes were on him as he rode past the defenders. Almost immediately Frank Haxton came up alongside him on a sorrel.

"Damn you. I can't let the others think I'm a coward. May you burn in hellfire for this."

"Aren't you curious what he has to say?"

"Who cares? All I want is to shoot the vermin full of holes. Him and all his ilk."

Ojo Blanco's eyes were lit by a fierce gleam. They bored into Fargo like twin daggers, but more with amusement than hate. A grin quirked the Mimbre leader's lips. "My head yet hurts."

"You have a thick skull," Fargo glibly responded.

Ojo Blanco's eyes narrowed. "You are not a planter of seeds. Yet you fight with these other white-eyes? What are they to you?"

"The chief of the bluecoats sent me to ask them to leave," Fargo answered, "but they will not listen."

"The bluecoat chief is wise. This is Mimbre land." Ojo Blanco's flinty gaze switched to Frank Haxton. "This one is not so wise. I have watched him. He is less than the droppings of my horse."

"I resent that!" Haxton snapped. "And I'll thank you to talk to me, not him. I can speak for myself."

"You will soon die, white-eye. You and all those with you. This will be Mimbre land again."

Hatred contorted Haxton's features. "Was that why you brought us out here? To threaten us?"

"I speak with a straight tongue. My people will take blood for blood. We will have vengeance for the two women and the children you killed."

"What?" Fargo said.

"You did not know? Ask this one." Ojo Blanco nodded at Haxton. "He was there. He and other whites shot them."

Fargo twisted in the saddle. "You stupid son of a bitch."

Haxton shrugged. "It was the first day we arrived. Two squaws and their brats were camped by the stream. They ran off, or tried to. We couldn't let them tell the rest of their tribe about us."

"So you *killed* them?"

Ojo Blanco answered instead. "This one and his friends shot them in the back as they ran. One boy hid in the woods. When the whites stopped hunting for him, he stole a horse. He was my sister's son. He died in my arms."

Fargo's trigger finger twitched.

"I did what was best for my people," Haxton defended himself. "How was I to know one of the gnats got away? I would do it again if I had it to do over."

Ojo Blanco's frame quivered like an aspen leaf in a storm, yet his demeanor was one of icy calm. "I remember," he said slowly in his thickly accented English, "when this land was only Mimbre land. I remember when there were no white men in this country. I remember when there were *Shis-Inday* and Navajos and Pimas, and Maricopas and other tribes, and a few Mexicans, but no white men. Life was good. The Mimbres were happy."

Frank Haxton snickered.

"Now many whites have come. The bluecoats with their guns. Whites like this one who dig at the ground. White villages of wood and stone. More whites keep coming. Soon there will be so many they will outnumber my people and all the other tribes."

"That we will!" Haxton crowed. "Your land will be our land and we will do with it as we please."

Ojo Blanco did not seem to hear him. "Our life is not as good as it was. My people are not as happy. They want the whites gone. But we have not made open war on the whites. Until now." He pointed a finger at Haxton. "You have killed our women. You have killed our children. You have taken our land. But this day it ends. This day the Mimbres say to the whites, no more."

"That's some speech, redskin," Frank Haxton said. "But you have it wrong. On this day the whites say to the Mimbres, this valley is ours to keep. We say this valley will run red with Mimbre blood."

Ojo Blanco turned to Fargo. "You may go. You struck me, but my quarrel is not with you. You do not take Mimbre land. You do not kill Mimbre women and children."

The offer caught Fargo off guard. Apaches seldom let an enemy live when it was within their power to do otherwise. The only explanation he could think of was that Ojo Blanco was doing it to spite Haxton. "I can't," he said.

"The woman from the canyon?"

"Her, and other things." Fargo did not elaborate.

"You may take her with you. We will not attack you. You have the word of Ojo Blanco."

Fargo was deeply moved. He considered accepting for Tricia's sake. She had not done anything to deserve to share the imminent fate of the settlers.

"Take her and go," Frank Haxton urged. "My daughter and I don't always see eye to eye, but she is flesh born of my flesh. Save her if you can."

Ojo Blanco's brow furrowed. "I did not know the woman is of his blood," he said to Fargo, "but I have given my word you may leave with her, and I do not speak with two tongues."

"I am grateful," Fargo said sincerely. "Ojo Blanco is generous. I wish I could accept. But I can't."

"I understand."

"Is this all you wanted?" Frank Haxton impatiently demanded.

"No." Ojo Blanco kneed his horse up next to Haxton's, and Haxton recoiled and raised an arm to ward off a blow that never came. "Do not fear. I will not kill you now. I wanted to look you in the eyes and tell you that soon you will die, *pindah lickoyee*. You will see your friends die. You will see your woman die. You will see that which you have built with your hands burned to the ground. You will see the crops you have grown burnt. You will see your cows killed and your horses killed and your dogs killed. You will see all this, and more, and then I will kill you with these." He raised his two hands. "I wanted you to know all this so you will be sick in your heart, as I and my people have been sick in ours."

"Do your worst, you red scum!" Frank Haxton snarled. "But it is you who will suffer this day!"

"Will I?" And Ojo Blanco looked over his shoulder and smiled.

Every other farmhouse in the valley was on fire. Every other barn was ablaze. Every shed and outhouse. Fields had been set on fire and the flames were spreading. Two-thirds of Paradise Valley was covered in a gigantic cloud of smoke, which was slowly being pushed northward by the vagrant breeze. It would be a while yet before it covered the entire valley, but the outcome was as plain to Fargo as chalk writing on a slate.

It wasn't plain to Frank Haxton. As arrogant as ever, he wheeled his mount and barked in parting, "We'll be waiting, redskin. Come and die if you want. I will happily send you to hell."

"Are many white-eyes as he is?" Ojo Blanco asked.

"Some. A lot, maybe," Fargo allowed. "Kill him and others will come to take his place. Not tomorrow or next month, but they will come."

"So be it, as you whites like to say." Ojo Blanco smiled. "We are warriors, you and I. We live as we must. We do what we must. You are my enemy but I respect you. He is my enemy and he is not worthy of respect." He said something in the Mimbre tongue to the other Mimbre and they started to turn their horses. "Until we meet again. May my knife prove quicker than yours."

Fargo was left by himself. He saw other Apaches watching, scores and scores of them, in large and small groups staggered the width of the valley, awaiting the signal that would precipitate the carnage.

The farmers were girding for battle. Extra ammunition was being passed out. More bales were being brought from the barn. Furniture from the house was being added to the barrier. Fred Haxton oversaw everything, bellowing like a general.

Calvin Peters was strangely quiet. He went about the tasks assigned to him, and when he was done, walked over to the corner of the barn where Fargo had stationed himself. "We need to talk about my wife."

"Nothing happened between us," Fargo reiterated, which was true so long as it only applied to the time since he arrived.

"Not that," Calvin said, and looked about to be sure no one could overhear. "I love her. I want her to live. When the time comes, get her out of here."

Surprise was piling on surprise. Fargo rejoined with, "You're her husband. It's for you to do."

"I might not be able to," Calvin said quietly. "I can't run out on the others. I'm Frank's second-in-command."

"I can't make any promises. Hell, I might not be able to get out myself."

"Try. I know we haven't seen eye to eye, and I haven't treated you right, but I'm man enough to own up to my mistakes, and I made one by letting Frank fill my head with tales of how glorious life here would be."

"You don't owe him anything."

"I owe myself. I owe the others." The big farmer clasped his big hands. "Please. I'm begging you, and I have never begged anyone for anything my whole life. Do what you can to save her. You're the only one who possibly can."

Fargo went into the barn. Horses were jammed in the stalls and the aisles, many still saddled. He selected two of the best and brought them to the front of the barn with the Ovaro. When he came back out, the first thing that struck him was the complete and total silence. No one was talking. No one moved. The farmers were riveted to the cloud of smoke, a gray shroud that stretched from the ground to high in the sky. It had crept to within a hundred yards of the south perimeter.

"Where did the Apaches get to?" a man wondered.

"I can't see a damn thing," another said.

Trimble could, from the barn roof. "The Mimbres are moving about! They're up to something!"

Frank Haxton climbed onto some bales of hay and raised an arm aloft. "Prepare to fire a volley on my command! Take aim!"

"At what?" Broder shouted.

"Shoot into the smoke," Haxton directed. "We're bound to hit something!" He surveyed the gleaming row of Henrys to his right and left, then slashed his arm down and roared, "Fire!"

Rifles cracked all along the line. Off in the smoke horses whinnied and one uttered a strangled cry.

"I told you!" Haxton beamed. "Fire at will! Keep at it until I tell you to stop! We'll show these ungodly bastards a thing or two!"

Lead and smoke belched in a torrent. The farmers fired as rapidly as they could work their Henrys, in an unending cascade of nigh-deafening thunder.

Fargo did not take part. The cloud was now only sixty yards away, and the wind had increased. He had maybe two minutes before the rabid wolves of revenge were unleashed. Running to the house, he entered without knocking. Fear-filled eyes focused on him, mothers and children alike sensing what he knew to be a certainty. "Tricia?" he shouted, and received an answer from down a narrow hall.

It led to the kitchen. She was at the stove, placing a pot of water on to boil. "For soup," she said at his questioning glance. "Some of the children are hungry."

"We're leaving."

"Now?"

Fargo grabbed her wrist and hurried back along the hall. "Danette Peters. Where is she?"

"Upstairs, I think," Tricia said. "In one of the bedrooms."

"Stay here." Fargo took the stairs three at a stride. The rifle fire outside had risen to a crescendo that could not drown out an undercurrent of lusty curses and shrieks. War whoops compounded the bedlam.

Danette was in the third bedroom, with other women and four children. Fargo looked at them and felt his insides churn. "You wanted out, didn't you?"

Perched on the edge of the bed, her hands clasped in her lap, her head hung low in despair, Danette gave a start and jumped to her feet. "Skye!"

"It's now or never," Fargo said. From the uproar outside, it might already be too late.

"You'll take me? After how I treated you?" Danette dashed to him and hugged him. "Yes! Yes! A thousand times yes! And don't worry about Calvin. He'll be too busy to notice us."

Downstairs, a woman screamed. Glass shattered, and there were hysterical shrieks and wails. Fargo went down in three long bounds.

An Apache had hurled a rocking chair from the front porch through a front window and was in the parlor. He had knocked down two women and had hold of a third by the front of her dress. In his other hand was a knife.

Fargo drew and fired from the hip, a snap shot that cored the warrior's forehead. He did not break stride. Grabbing Tricia, he wrenched the door open and was ten feet into the yard before his mind absorbed the riotous chaos raging on all sides. The Haxton farm had become a maelstrom of blood-drenched ferocity.

The smoke had reached the south barrier. So had the Mimbres. Warriors and settlers were embroiled in brutal conflict. Henrys and revolvers boomed. Bowstrings twanged. Cold steel plunged into torsos. Empty rifles were wielded like clubs. Fists and knees and teeth were employed when all else was in vain. Here a farmer blew out the brains of an Apache scrambling onto a wagon. There a warrior nearly decapitated a white-eye with a single stroke of a keen-edged blade. Violence piled on violence in a whirlwind, crimson mosaic. Men fell on both sides, some wounded but fighting on, others abruptly nipped in the bud of life, dead before they realized they had been shot or stabbed or bashed.

Women were firing from the windows of the house, but there were not enough of them to make a difference. They missed more than they hit, and the warriors they hit did not always drop. Mimbres were rushing the ground floor. Some had gained entry and were wreaking havoc.

Fargo steeled himself against the cries. There was not a damn thing he could do to help them. He would only get himself killed. Choked with emotion, he raced for the barn, Tricia and Danette close behind.

Danette screeched when a brawny Apache rushed them, nocking an arrow to a sinew string. Fargo's Colt sped a slug more swiftly than the shaft could fly, and the warrior pitched to the grass in a scarlet smear.

"Almost there!" Fargo yelled, even though they couldn't hear him above the madhouse pandemonium. He reached the open door and turned just as an arrow flashed out of the spreading gray veil and transfixed Danette Peters's neck from left to right. She jolted to a halt, her eyes wide in incredulity, her hands rising to the shaft. They never touched it. Blood spurted from her mouth and her nostrils and oozed down both sides of her neck, and she died on her feet, her eyelids fluttering like the gossamer wings of a stricken butterfly.

Tricia had stopped and was staring in blank horror at Danette's final throes.

"Come on!" Fargo seized her arm and propelled her into the barn. The horses were prancing and nickering and some were ready to bolt. He heaved her onto her mount, then swung onto the Ovaro. "Can you ride?"

Nodding numbly, Tricia licked her lips.

They broke from the barn at a gallop. Fighting figures filled the yard, combat at its most fierce, white men and red men locked in grimly macabre dances of death.

Fargo reined due north. The defenders on that side had rushed to the aid of those to the south and the way was clear—or should be. But out of the veil appeared a long line of mounted Apaches. He drew rein and aimed the Colt, but he did not shoot.

At the center of the line was Ojo Blanco. He motioned, and the warriors to his left parted, forming a path.

Tricia had frozen in terror. Fargo snatched her reins and jabbed his spurs. He did not glance back until they were well beyond the Mimbres, and he was sorry he did. The sanguinary spectacle would be seared into his memory for as long as he lived. Bodies were everywhere. Pools of red marked the green. Flames licked at the farmhouse, and from it came the most terrible screams the human ear ever heard.

One sight in particular stood out—that of Frank Haxton, his hands flung out in stark terror, hemmed by Mimbres on horseback as a stocky avenger stalked toward him.

Fargo rode faster and did not look back again.

LOOKING FORWARD!
The following is the opening
section of the next novel in the exciting
Trailsman series from Signet:

THE TRAILSMAN #296
SIX-GUN PERSUASION

Northwest Arkansas, 1860—where murder is epidemic and Fargo is dispensing the cure—up to six pills per dose.

Yet another crackling volley of gunfire echoed through the timbered hill country of northwest Arkansas, reminding the crop-bearded, buckskin-clad rider that the Wild West began almost the moment a man crossed the Mississippi.

Skye Fargo reined in, removing his hat to whack at the flies buzzing around his head. He had spent most of his life desperately trying to avoid the net of civilization, but it was being cast everywhere these days. He patiently studied the surrounding terrain, a patchwork quilt of wooded hills and grassy flats, with the vast Ozark Plateau to the north and mountains visible to the south. He was riding along a narrow divide, the high ground between two valleys.

Fargo's sun-slitted, lake blue eyes were especially vigilant for the glint of rifle barrels. Ragged parcels of cloud drifted across a sky of china blue. It was late summer, with the area deep into a dry spell, and most of the small farmers were running hard just to stand still. The hills, scarred by deep washes, still teemed with sweet clover, though the grass—including crucial pasturage—was yellow-brown from the drought.

"This region's always had its troubles, old campaigner," Fargo remarked quietly to his Ovaro. "But lately, it's become hell turned inside out."

The violence in Arkansas was worse than Fargo had ever seen it. If the Great Plains, beginning just to the west, were the wide front door of the West, then Arkansas was part of the hard threshold. Just north of here, the famous westward trails began, at St. Joseph and Independence, Missouri. Arkansas, like Missouri, was a stepping-off place, a lawless borderland with gangs, and even armies, of kill-crazy marauders controlling everyone and everything.

"Well, now, *here's* a tonic," Fargo remarked, perking up and slapping the dust from his buckskins.

A young woman on foot, carrying a sewing basket over one arm, was approaching from behind, headed in the same direction Fargo was riding. Fargo, who sampled women like bees sampled flowers, immediately recognized this gal as a top-shelf sample. A long, fair oval of face peered out from under beribboned russet curls, and perpetually pursed lips egged a man on to kiss them. She wore a pretty, form-flattering dress of sprigged muslin. Nor was this the usual poor hoe-man's daughter—a gold brooch fastened her collar of crocheted lace.

"Hey, long shanks!" she greeted Fargo with a saucy smile. "You get lost from your wagon train? A body can see at a glance you ain't the type to grub taters."

She sashayed past Fargo and stopped in the rutted trail to study him with bold, approving eyes the color of dark berries. Fargo, in turn, leaned forward and rested his muscular forearms on the saddle horn, studying her right back.

"Ain't *you* bold?" she chided without anger as the tall stranger drank her in.

"You can't hang a man for his thoughts," Fargo reminded her.

"Mr. Buckskins, I wouldn't even put *you* on trial," she assured him. "Wild and woolly and hard to curry, I bet. My name, by the way, is Mary Lou Tutt."

"Pleased to meetcha, Mary Lou. The name's Skye Fargo."

"A body don't see fellows of your cut very much around here, Skye," she told him. A shadow crossed her face as a thought occurred to her. "Unless . . . you been sent in to do some killing?"

"From what I can see, Arkansas needs to hire killers like Texas needs to hire prairie dogs."

Even as Fargo fell silent, more gunshots crackled in the distance, making his point.

"It's all because of slavery," Mary Lou said, bitterness edging into her voice. "All a body hears these days is talk about a horrible war coming."

Fargo nodded. The trouble began in earnest with the opening of the Kansas Territory in 1854 and the turbulent question: free or slave? The actual Border War was triggered two years later when fanatical abolitionist John Brown and three of his sons savagely murdered and mutilated five pro-slavery men. With talk of a great civil war now brewing, the battle had become the Kansas abolitionists or Jayhawkers, "Free Staters," versus the Missouri "Border Ruffians," pro-slavers.

Both sides used the slavery issue as an excuse to kill and plunder. Arkansas got sucked into the mess by virtue of its crucial location and high number of caves. Pro-slavery gangs, often drunk, patrolled the country, harassing all would-be settlers. Not surprisingly, new arrivals formed their own militia bands for self-defense—and now armed bands were everywhere, thick as ticks on a hound.

"It's got so confused," Fargo told Mary Lou, "that

troops sent in to restore order end up fighting both factions. Up in Kansas, the new governor just resigned in outright fear for his life. Hell, on my way here I saw at least a thousand Border Ruffians encamped on the Missouri-Arkansas line. The U.S. Army couldn't muster even half that number out here—not with war building back east."

"Pukes," Mary Lou said, her voice harsh with contempt as she used the popular name for the Border Ruffians. "Puttin' colored folks in chains and callin' themselves Christians. It's a sin to Moses."

However, Fargo noticed a glint of sudden suspicion in those berry-juice eyes. "Skye, you seem to know plenty about the army and such. Is that why you're here—sent in by the army for a look-see?"

Fargo laughed, strong white teeth flashing through his beard. "You sure are a *wary* lass," he teased her. "What's a pretty young thing like you so afraid of?"

"If you lived around here, you'd know."

"Well, you can rest easy about me. I sometimes work for the army, sure, but only as a civilian contract scout. Matter fact, I just finished three months work out in the Far West for the War Department's Corps of Topographical Engineers."

"Topo-*who*?" she cut in. "Laws, that's a mouthful."

"Mapmakers," he explained, grinning. "We mapped the Black Rock Desert in northern Utah Territory and parts of the Humboldt River country."

"That's sure a far piece from Arkansas," she reminded him.

"I'm here because, after my contract expired, I came across a small party of emigrants from west Tennessee. They'd been attacked by Comanches in New Mexico Territory, half of them killed or wounded. The survivors wanted no part of the West and begged me to guide them back home. There were several kids along, so I took everybody back to Tennessee. Now my needle points west again. I'm headed toward Pikes Peak country."

The suspicion eased from Mary Lou's face and was replaced by disappointment.

"So you won't be staying in Lead Hill very long?" she asked, her tone urging him to reconsider.

"Lead Hill?" he repeated. "Not a very reassuring name. Never heard of it."

Again a pensive frown transformed her pretty face. "Oh, it's aptly named, for a surety. Lies straight ahead about two miles. Place ain't been there long, though."

Fargo wasn't surprised. Jerkwater towns were springing up all over this part of the West—so called because many of them were water stops where the train crews jerked a chain to lower the waterspout over the boiler.

"Lead Hill got a livery or a blacksmith?" Fargo asked her.

She nodded. "Romer Wiltz runs both."

Fargo was in a pinch. He had foolishly trusted a drunk blacksmith back in Batesville, and now his stallion's right rear shoe had been clicking for several miles. Bad shoeing lamed more horses than anything else, and unless the shoe was pulled and reset immediately, the pinto would almost surely founder—and Fargo's hasp and shoeing hammer had been stolen from his saddlebags in Tennessee.

"I require the services of this Romer Wiltz," Fargo told Mary Lou. "How 'bout you, pretty lady? Headed to town?"

"Ain't exactly a town, but sure, I'm headed there to leave some work for the seamstress. And I *do* ride horseback in a dress, case you're offering to take me."

"Be glad to . . . take you," Fargo punned with a sly grin, swinging down to help this tasty little country tidbit into the saddle.

"Glad? Oh, I guarantee you'd be powerful glad, Mr.

Buckskins," she promised in a voice gone husky. "So why'n't you stay around awhile?"

Fargo hadn't done the mazy waltz in weeks, and this Arkansas beauty was definitely a suitable nubile prospect. Her frank talk already had him aroused. He swung her up into leather, pleasantly aware of her ample breasts pressuring his back, her moist, warm breath on his neck.

They had barely gotten under way, Fargo holding the Ovaro to an easy trot, when the rataplan of racing hooves approached from behind. Fargo sent a cross-shoulder glance to the rear and saw a coal black stallion racing toward them, his rider whipping him to a lather with a leather quirt.

"Oh, Moses on the mountain!" Mary Lou fretted, her grip on Fargo's midsection tightening in fear. "Skye, I am *so* sorry!"

"Why? That your husband or beau?"

"Huh! Neither one. That's Clay Evans coming, and he's a mite tetched—his whole clan is. You might say he's set his cap for me—his *night*cap. But he means to kill me after he rapes me."

Fargo had more questions, but right now he had to get set for possible trouble. He reined right, clearing the trail for Clay Evans, and then knocked the riding thong off the hammer of his belt gun. He left his palm resting on the butt of the Colt, but didn't clear leather. It was as volatile here as anywhere else in the West, and a man had to be very careful about filling his hand. Fargo had seen too many pissing fights end in a coil of blue gun smoke.

However, the rider never even slackened his pace. Fargo glimpsed a strapping, hatless young man in his early twenties, with a round, flushed face and hair black as licorice, slicked back with axle grease. Many young men of this turbulent area were not considered criminals, but rather, "harum-scarum"—reckless and unpredictable. The look in this man's eyes, however, when they met Fargo's, was unmistakably murderous.

Excerpt from SIX-GUN PERSUASION

The moment Clay Evans switched his reins to his left hand, freeing his gun hand, Fargo skinned out his Colt quicker than eyesight. Since Evans hadn't actually drawn, Fargo merely held the shooter ready for action but not aimed.

For a moment, Evans stared in disbelief, perhaps wondering how that gun got into Fargo's fist so rapidly. Whatever he'd planned, he again took the reins in both hands. Now his attention shifted to Mary Lou.

"Two-bit whore!" he insulted her as he thundered past. He included Fargo in the insult when he added, "I see you hump trail trash now! Got tired of Injins and darkies, huh?"

"Murdering scum!" she threw after him. "Killed a child today?"

"Oh, Jesus," Fargo said, figuring out the clues. "The Tutts and the Evanses are feuding, right?"

"You just keep your nose out of the pie," she snapped, still seething with anger. "And be mighty careful, hear? Now he's seen you with me, he'll be down on you like all wrath."

"His choice," Fargo said calmly, sliding the thong over the hammer and kneeing the Ovaro forward. That "trail trash" remark had been duly noted and filed away. "I'll be having a little discussion with him, I expect."

"Skye, don't you dare! You'll catch a weasel asleep before you ever talk any sense into that no-account Evans trash."

"His choice," Fargo said again. "Me, I'm a lovable cuss. That's it, darlin'. Hang on tight."

"Like this, Skye? Or is my left hand too low?"

An ear-to-ear smile divided Fargo's bearded, weather-bronzed face. "*Just* like that, Miss Mary Lou."

No other series has this much historical action!

THE TRAILSMAN